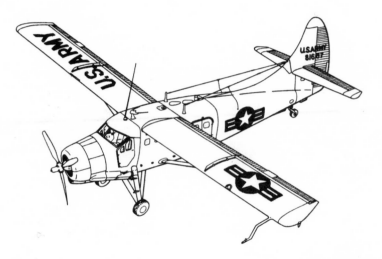

de Havilland U-1A Otter

*D*ANGEROUS
*P*AST

A. F. EBBERS

SILVERHAWK BOOKS   *MANCHACA, TEXAS*

Published by:
SILVERHAWK BOOKS
P.O. Box 2284
Manchaca, TX 78652-2284
www.silverhawkbooks.com

FIRST EDITION

10 9 8 7 6 5 4 3 2 1

This novel is a work of fiction. Events and characters depicted are fictitious and any resemblance to actual persons, living or dead, is purely coincidental and is the product of the author's creation.

ISBN-13: 978-0-9789482-3-8
ISBN-10: 0-9789482-3-8

Printed in the United States of America

ACKNOWLEDGEMENTS

I have many people to thank for help in assisting me on this book. First and foremost I have to give special kudos to Walter J. Boyne, the former director of the National Air & Space Museum at the Smithsonian and founder of the prominent *Air & Space Magazine*. A *New York Times* best selling author of fifty books and numerous articles, including the renowned novel, *The Wild Blue,* a busier man I couldn't conceive, yet he took the time to review my chapters and gave me, a first novelist, an acclaim.

Along those same lines, Airline Captain Gary Prosser, at my request, carefully reviewed my airliner in distress chapter and pointed out some vital things I hadn't included. As a senior captain in the B747 with a major airline, he is also qualified as a captain in the DC10, B777, B737, and B727 among many others, and I think you will appreciate his expertise in that chapter.

Thanks is also due for David Bitterman, a Gulfstream IV jet captain, who gave me some valuable and updated advice on handling today's large jet aircraft.

Special thanks goes to St. Edward's University English professor and Librarian Fran Ebbers, who also happens to be my editor-in-chief and wife, who read and re-read *Dangerous Past* at least a hundred times over the past several years. Her corrections and suggestions and occasional patience were invaluable.

Special thanks also to professional reader Alison Carpenter for a last minute look to weed out those always invisible typos or missed words.

The author also wishes to thank those writing professors who put up with me over the decades, and the attendants at Hamilton Pool Park Preserve who answered all my probing questions and a special thanks to the Adjutant General's Staff of the Texas Army National Guard who took time to explain military criminal law.

Special appreciation goes to Rebecca Duncan, who did a magnificent job on the cover art and to Terry Sherrell for typesetting *Dangerous Past.*

And what can I offer but appreciation to relatives and for their specialties like expert computer consultant and son-in-law Ron Whitson and his graphic suggestions for a cover, and his wife, Carolyn, attorney and former high school English teacher and my daughter, who gave me a thumbs up read on my manuscript's characters.

DEDICATION

Army Aviation cannot boast of a blueblood heritage. It started with a few dozen Piper Cubs in 1942. Without traditions to follow or carloads of military flying regulations to hinder capabilities, it grew by 1970 to 12,000 aircraft and 24,000 pilots to have at that time, a larger air fleet than the United States Air Force. In Vietnam, with helicopters and planes akin to those flown in general aviation, they carried more passengers, hauled more tons of cargo, flew more hours of combat, and, consequently, lost more pilots than its brethren in the other air services. The Huey helicopter alone saved countless lives of the foot soldiers. It's to those Army aircrews that this book is dedicated.

"All that is necessary for the triumph of evil is that good men do nothing."

— Edmund Burke

PROLOGUE

Vietnam 1967

Water poured from dirty clouds as though the South China Sea was overhead. An American army sergeant crouched in a 6-foot thicket of elephant grass and ferns ignored the raindrops cascading off the bill of his cap. He stiffened when he heard the distant sound of a vehicle engine. Reaching down to his webbed belt, he unsnapped the leather cover to a Colt .45-caliber pistol.

A quarter mile away, the skinny imposter behind the wheel of the three-quarter ton Army truck never gave a thought to slowing down even though the downpour obstructed his vision and the underbrush threatened to swallow his only pathway.

He bounced along the muddy trail in perpetual motion, much like his lifestyle, savoring the chameleon roles he played.

Abruptly the trail ended, causing the driver to brake hard. The vehicle skidded on the wet ground into a clearing the size of a tennis court. Several feet away a circular pond of black liquid stood out like a dark blotch on a green carpet. He had found the deep bomb crater four miles north of the Nha Trang airbase where his unit has been illegally dumping used aviation oil.

Only three months ago as an Army CID agent, Jack Braden had posed as a dining facility sergeant at Ft. Benning, flushing out details of a mysterious mess hall fire half a year earlier. It had been his best performance yet. Nobody had been happier than the cooks when the Army had to build an updated mess facility to replace the burned out ruins. But few would talk about it. So he stole a pickle jar containing $101 from a freezer. Military police were called in to investigate the theft of the party funds. The kitchen workers were more than willing to take lie detector tests to show that they didn't steal the money.

The tests got results, especially when the lie detector operator asked, "Were you involved in the mess hall fire?" Within the hour the arson case was solved. Now he was assigned to Vietnam, impersonating an enlisted aviation company clerk named Pat Burnside.

But he wasn't within the safe confines of an orderly room office now, and Jack hesitated before leaving the truck cab, looking carefully around the area. The last thing he wanted to see was another human face. As he peered out the windshield at the desolation, his right heel tapped rapidly against the floorboard. He knew there were no sanctuaries in Vietnam and to him this locale looked about as safe as an isolated footpath in New York's Central Park at midnight.

In the dense foliage several feet from where Jack sat in his truck, a figure watched silently.

After determining that he was alone, Jack turned off his engine, grabbed his M16 rifle and stepped down from the cab. The steady downpour had finally yielded to a clinging drizzle. He walked quickly to the rear of the vehicle and lowered the tailgate. Laying his weapon inside the truck body, he pulled several five-gallon metal cans from the canvas-covered interior and carried them two at a time to the edge of the pond. He was careful where he placed his feet. The crater, he was told, was 10 to 12 feet deep and slipping into it would be like falling into quicksand.

In a few minutes he carried the final two cans to the edge of the pond. Jack knew he could get the unit cited for improper disposal of used oil. But that would be inconsequential when compared to the real transgression he had uncovered. He reflected that not only the company but the whole damn country was the perfect place for those on the take.

The concealed sergeant edged his big frame forward in a semi-crouch until the elephant grass snapped in protest. He froze, waiting for a reaction from Jack. There was none. Then he started moving again, violating the stillness of the area.

To Jack, the initial noise had resembled wind rustling through leaves. Only there wasn't any breeze at the moment. The sound repeated itself. Jack dropped the oil cans and jerked upright. Heart pounding, he whirled and scanned the area. He listened intently, hearing only his own heavy breathing. Maybe it was a monkey, a bird or one of those fat-as-a-cat rodents that populated the country. The hair on his arms rose when he heard the sound again. Before he could dash back to the safety of his rifle, a familiar voice commanded, "Burnside."

The vegetation parted and he saw the maintenance sergeant who had ordered him to dispose of the oil. Beyond the path that the sergeant had made through the underbrush, Jack saw the silhouette of another figure sitting in a jeep. Since he had not heard the jeep motor he knew that they had arrived before him.

"Jesus, you scared me." Jack took a deep breath. "What brings you out here?"

The sergeant stepped out into the open. His clothing clung to him like wet fur. He looked towards Jack but not directly at him. His eyes, devoid of expression, were focused on the agent's forehead or perhaps just beyond. It was hard to tell.

Jack started wiping his hands with an oil rag rapidly. The man standing before him, one of the suspects in his investigation and the most dangerous one, had once called Jack the most efficient clerk in the Army. Now he acted as if he knew Jack's true identity.

The sergeant, rigid, silent, thin lips remaining tight under a protruding nose, eyes still vacant, resembled a drenched, skin-covered robot.

Jack snapped his fingers, "Dammit, I left a can in the truck." But he got no further than his first step when the sergeant withdrew the pistol from his holster and mechanically slid the metallic housing on top of the barrel back and forth, chambering a round. Waving the pistol, he motioned for Jack to stop.

In desperation, Jack looked toward the other figure in the jeep. He could faintly make out captain's bars on the man's uniform. But the officer turned his head away, leaving Jack as queasy as if he had inhaled a cheap cigar on an empty stomach. He again tried to make eye contact with the sergeant. "Hey, let's talk. We can work something out."

The sergeant didn't respond as he raised the pistol head-high, moving closer to Jack, trapping his victim between the pond and himself.

"Think—Don't use that on me. . . ." Jack spoke rapidly now, beseechingly, backing toward the oil pit and holding his arms out to ward off the assassin who was taking aim at Jack's head. "DON'T SHOO—."

Jack's words, hopes and future became history as the first of the two big slugs sent pieces of his skull flying.

Late that night in the orderly room of the 119th Aviation Company, First Sergeant Elmer Clyde, 50, a rawboned 'lifer' from the poverty belt of the southern Appalachian Mountains, and the company's Executive Officer, Captain Miles Fenton, sat at Clyde's desk.

"I'll see to it that Burnside is reported as AWOL when he fails to show up for the morning formation. Eventually, people will think the VC got him."

"Or maybe not," Clyde said with a worried frown.

"I'd call it a dead issue," Fenton said with a smirk on his face.

Clyde stared at Fenton, clearly not amused at the XO's attempt at levity.

Clyde could be called a holdover from the old brown shoe Army. Everything in the First Sergeant's office was standard Army—harsh and sparse—except for the sergeant's upholstered executive chair, obviously obtained from another source. The plush chair seemed to reflect the personality of its occupant—a man in charge. Clyde leaned back in his throne and waited for a more reassuring answer from Fenton.

"Relax," Fenton said. *These ancient Army sergeants are more cautious than old maids.* It's easy to see why he was never officer material.

"It's not just Burnside. We can't go around just killing CID agents. They'll send more until they get the evidence they want."

"Don't worry. Apparently they don't have anything or know who's involved and probably not even sure if anything illegal is going on.

Fenton, whom other officers in the company referred to as Captain Cocky, continued, "Burnside never had time to get a report back to them. The Army's CID lost agents before to the VC. Hell, this is a war zone."

Clyde sifted uncomfortably in his seat, his eyes reflecting doubt.

"If another spook shows up, you just assign him to one of our platoons so far away from our operation that he'll rotate home before he gets within a hundred miles of the First Platoon. Besides, we got George to handle it" Fenton said, as he dusted off a polished boot on the edge of Clyde's desk.

Clyde glared at the boot on his desk. "George is another thing we need to talk about. We got to keep him on a leash or he's going to get us all hanged."

"Poor George, our maligned maintenance sergeant. He's as harmless as a pissed off Pit Bull," Fenton said mockingly.

"He's a psycho if I ever saw one," Clyde snapped.

"Take it easy. Who else do we have who's willing to get rid of our dirty laundry? Besides," Fenton pointed at the First Sergeant, "with the money you're making from this operation, your complaint sounds a little bit hypocritical."

The one thing that Fenton respected most was money, lots of it—and he was willing to take risks to get it. And he didn't like whiners. Like his late father, a disbarred probate attorney who specialized in cheating inheritors out of their inheritance, Fenton always had a nose for moneymaking schemes. In college, he would sneak into professors' offices at night and photocopy final exam questions to sell to other students.

As a university student he made out greatly with young, very young ladies. During summer breaks, he would bring home a small box full of fraternity pledge pins and distribute them individually to high school girls with promises of undying love to gain their intimate favors. Highly intelligent, completely unethical, and with plenty of street smarts he would've made lots of money as a civilian if he hadn't got involved with ROTC and received an Army commission.

Sergeant Clyde sat with a deadpan expression on his face, and much to Fenton's disgust, nervously started picking at his nose. "You know as we get near our departure DEROS date, Lan will also be a big problem."

"How?"

"He could blackmail our asses for the rest of our lives, even if we're back in the States."

"Hmm. I believe you have a point, sergeant. But killing him shouldn't be too hard. Not with all the cutthroats available in Laos. Besides, that would save me about ten grand."

"How's that," Clyde said.

"Lan couldn't make our last meeting with the Corsicans to get his share of the payment for the load of poppies we delivered the previous week, and he looked worried. To calm him down, I gave him my IOU for the amount. So, the fool is holding a worthless piece of paper if we dispatch him to Oriental heaven," Fenton said grinning.

"Hell, knowing you, it's worthless even if we didn't get rid of him," Clyde said flatly.

1

October, 2000

The air was smooth as the Boeing 737-200 airliner sliced gracefully east through the night autumn sky over southern Tennessee. Letters scripted in dark blue printed out the name WestSky across the sides of its white fuselage.

On the flight deck, Captain Frank Braden, 50, a fellow with inquisitive brown eyes, salt-and-pepper hair and easy-going mannerisms, occupied the left seat.

First Officer John Tate, 30, an eager-to-please copilot, is in the right seat. Tate had been delighted to see that he was scheduled to fly with Braden. Frank was known as a less demanding captain on his copilots and was easy to get along with, unlike a few captains who turned into hard-to-please tyrants in the cockpit. But he also knew that Braden was nobody's fool and insisted on professionalism in the cockpit at all times.

"Heard you flew in 'Nam?" Tate said.

Frank eyed his younger flight companion before answering, "For a short while."

"Not a full year?"

"Got shot and sent back to the States."

"Bummer. Viet Cong?"

Again, Frank hesitated before answering. "No. American."

The First Officer's interest visually perked up. "Wow, that's cool. I mean, not you getting shot, but an American shooting you. Never heard of that happening."

And, thankfully, my life has been mundane even since, Frank reflected.

"You know, I was just starting grade school when 'Nam was going on."

Frank nodded.

Tate paused and anxiously waited for his captain to follow-up the shooting episode with an explanation. But only silence penetrated the cockpit. Out of the corner of his eye the First Officer saw his Captain staring blankly at the dark outside world beyond the windshield.

Frank knew he had little to complain about, even with his recent stock losses. Everything he had worked hard for he had achieved. As a senior captain with a major airline and married to a prominent and attractive surgeon, he figured they could get out of bankruptcy within two years. But then what? His two kids were in college and ready to leave home, and his wife recently starting spending more time at medical conventions and hospitals than at home. Sometimes they rarely talked when they were home together. Basically, he was worried that his brainy wife might be bored with him for not paying more attention to her. Was she thinking of splitting?

"Everything okay, skipper?" Tate asked.

Frank, momentarily distracted from his isolated thoughts, turned to his copilot. "In the end, everything works out for the best, doesn't it?"

Not sure how to answer, Tate ventured, "I guess it does." John Tate was not one to disagree with any captain he was flying with even though he may not have completely understood the question. But he was not one to be able to contain his curiosity, either. He again abruptly broke the captain's solitude, "Why'd he shoot you?"

Frank looked down and picked up an approach plate booklet and examined it. The copilot finally got the hint and, although disappointed, wisely didn't pursue the questioning any further.

About a dozen feet behind and on the other side of the flight deck door in the First Class section, senior flight attendant Beth Jordan, mid-30s, smiled as she handed a cup of coffee to a rotund businessman. Beth, slim, with a pleasant personality, had been with WestSky for ten years. She had planned to leave the airline five years ago, but her husband's real estate business had its own recession and they needed the extra income.

"Cream or sugar?" She asked in a very polite but professional voice.

Suddenly, a terrific loud **BANG** shook the airliner like dynamite, tearing a ten by twelve-foot hole into the bottom right side of the aircraft fuselage. A deafening tornado-like wind rushed through the interior of the passenger cabin like a giant vacuum cleaner, sucking up anything not nailed or strapped down. Simultaneously, a brief, chilled mist swept through the cabin amid the screaming passengers whose voices could not be heard above the shrieking wind. Paper and debris floated everywhere. Speechless, the rotund businessman's body instantly became caught in the suction towards the hole. His body jerked upwards but was held by his seat belt. Stunned and scared, his eyes widened as they involuntarily followed the stewardess, coffee cups, papers and other

19

debris, down and out of the aircraft through a gaping hole in the bottom right front fuselage of the plane.

It had all happened so fast, even Beth didn't have a chance to scream, just wore a shocked expression on her face as she disappeared into the night.

Seconds later, the power of the giant vacuum dissipated as the cabin pressure equalized with the outside atmosphere. But dangling oxygen masks waved back and forth and a ceaseless, deafening, howling wind from the hole in the fuselage continued.

In the economy class, women continued to mouth unheard screams. A pair of flight attendants knocked to the aisle by the explosive decompression, grabbed the bottom supports of the seats and held on until suction towards the cavity ceased. Then they scrambled to their feet, motioning for everyone to put the masks on their faces. As if to demonstrate, they snatched two hanging masks from nearby empty seats and put them on.

Simultaneously, the same wind shrieked through the cockpit making normal conversation impossible. Debris, papers, checklists, and pieces of gray insulation floated everywhere.

"Shit," Tate yelled. But nobody heard him. The sound of the wind drowned him out.

Frank quickly donned his oxygen mask, disconnected the autopilot, retarded the power levers, held the control yoke slightly backwards and banked the aircraft to descend. He squinted at his copilot since the swirling debris made opening the eyes fully very dangerous. After seeing Tate put on his mask, he pointed to the intercom switch. Both men turned the switch on. Now they could hear each other through their oxygen mask mikes and headsets.

"Explosive decompression, emergency descent, I have the controls, extend the speed brakes," Frank said quickly.

Tate extended the speed brakes and put on the cabin seat belt sign.

The First Officer switched from intercom to air traffic control and in an unsettled voice, yelled into his oxygen mike, "Mayday. Mayday. Mayday. WestSky Flight two-five-three. Explosive decompression. One hundred ten souls on board. Thirty- thousand pounds of fuel. Leaving flight level three-three zero for one zero-zero now."

Frank pointed at the transponder. Tate nodded and put in the numbers, 7700, the emergency code.

"Can you see what's going on back there?" Frank said.

The copilot turned towards the rear and gasped. The cockpit door had been blown off its hinges and he saw the gaping hole in the aisle of the First Class passenger compartment.

"There's a hole in the bottom of the aircraft in First Class. I can see lights on the ground through it."

"See the attendants? How are the passengers?" Frank said rapidly.

"Beth's missing. The other attendants are getting off the floor in the rear cabin but they look okay."

"Passengers?"

"Scared. But they're in their seats sniffing oxygen." Tate looked for the emergency checklist but couldn't find it in the debris. So he did it by memory, mumbling to himself while he glanced at the control and instrument panels. "Captain — airspeed."

Frank looked at the rapidly unwinding clock-like altimeter and the increasing needle on the airspeed indicator and nodded. He pulled the yoke back a little further to decrease the airspeed a bit while still maintaining a rapid descent to breathable outside air. "Any reply from Memphis Center?"

Tate shook his head, "Can't hear a thing. Still too much noise."

"Keep transmitting in the blind. Tell 'em it's structural failure, vibrating badly. We're diverting to Memphis."

The airframe vibrations were quite noticeable as the airliner continued its descent. Tate, on a second look, reported that the interior of the fuselage near the tail section seemed to be moving slightly up and down on its own.

A dozen thoughts were racing through Frank's mind. *God, I hope the structure of this old bird holds together at this speed. Once the integrity of an airframe has been compromised, all bets are off. Dammit, there's no way to dump fuel from a 737 and we got a lot of it. At least we're still flying. So the worst is probably over. Hope we got good weather at Memphis.*

Out of the sight of the pilots, a small hanging piece of aluminum sheeting on the side bottom of the airline fuselage tore loose in the slipstream and slammed into the right engine inlet. Sparks flew out and a fire warning light ignited on the instrument panel.

Frank spotted the red light almost immediately. "God! What's next," Frank said to himself. He then yelled to Tate. "Check number two engine."

Tate didn't have to look hard. His eyes widened. An orange-reddish flume from the jet engine lit up the right side of the wing. Black heavy smoke trailed behind the engine.

"She's on fire."

"Damn." Frank quickly shut down the right engine and yelled to Tate. "Number two's down. Push the fire button."

Tate reached to the center console. He twisted a big red button marked No.2.

"If it doesn't go out give her another fire bottle in thirty seconds." Tate waited out the seconds and eagerly twisted the fire button again. He then switched on the right wing spotlight which he didn't need. His eyes widened. In a grim voice he said, "Still see flames. Smoking like hell, too."

"Tell Memphis we got one turning and one burning," Frank replied. He didn't want to even think about the possibility of the fire melting the engine support struts. He knew that a departing engine and pod would likely take a portion of the wing with it.

"Approaching ten thousand."

"Roger. Leveling off," Frank said. "Retract speed brakes."

As the aircraft slowed, the cockpit wind noise lessened. Tate slipped off his oxygen mask. Frank ripped his off with his one free hand.

The copilot looked uneasily at Frank. "I'm feeling more vibrations."

"Roger. Can't control her below 170 knots." Frank held the control yoke with both hands now, struggling to keep the aircraft from rolling either to the port or starboard sides. He nodded towards the power lever. "Reach over and give me a little more power on number one." Tate reached over and pushed the lever forward a little and the airspeed indicator increased to one hundred and eighty knots, dissipating the aircraft's tendency to roll but causing the vibrations to increase.

"That'll be our approach speed," Frank said.

A ground controller voice was heard in their headsets. "WestSky two-five-three. Do you read?"

"Got you five-by-five now. Get our transmissions?" Tate eagerly replied.

"Roger, flight two-five three. Air traffic at Memphis has been diverted. You're clear for a straight-in ILS approach to runway three six left. Ceiling 200. Fog. Visibility, quarter mile. Wind calm. Altimeter 2996."

Tate alternated between looking at the smoking engine, at the instrument panel and glancing out the front windshield. He didn't like anything he saw. Underneath them was a blanketing white sea of mist that they must descend their wobbling, burning, airliner into at high speed to reach safety. He felt himself getting nauseous thinking about their odds. Taking a deep breath, he looked for the approach plate manual and couldn't find it in the mess. He radioed their predicament to ATC. The controller answered in a minute giving frequencies and headings and altitudes required.

"Glideslope alive. You can start your descent," Tate said.

"Got it," Frank replied.

"I can still see flames coming from the engine," Tate said quietly.

"Roger," Frank said.

The controller voice was again heard over the headsets. "Emergency equipment is in position by the runway. Switch now to final controller on one-two-four point one-five. Good luck."

Before Tate could acknowledge a reply, Frank quickly injected an afterthought into the mike. "Keep the emergency vehicles away from the runway. With the structural damage we have we're not too sure how aerodynamic we might be on touchdown. Could cartwheel."

"I'll pass it on," the controller said.

While Tate changed radio frequencies, Frank gently pulled back the single power lever with his right hand and held a slight back pressure on the control yoke with his left hand as the crippled airliner descended into the murky fogbank seeking the safety of the runway two thousand feet below.

The vibrations lessened somewhat as the airspeed decreased but the wing alternately dipped and rose to one side or the other while Frank tried desperately to wrestle it back to the level position. He knew if the wing dropped just above the ground, the aircraft could cartwheel wing over wing, tearing itself into fractured pieces of metal in which only a lucky few would survive, if that many.

Flames and smoke continued pouring from the starboard engine, baggage occasionally dropping out from the gaping hole in its fuselage, as the Boeing 737 started the last approach its badly damaged airframe would ever make.

Frank glued his eyes to instruments on the panel, struggling to keep the wings level in the fog. Tate sat forward in his seat, beads of sweat on his forehead, his hand on the landing gear lever, his eyes trying to penetrate through the mist to see the runway.

"Vibrations increasing again," Tate warned.

As the Boeing 737 sped downward, Frank, eyeing the ILS indicator, kept the localizer and glide slope needles immobile.

"Descending thru 300 feet," Tate called out. "Runway not in sight."

We're coming in too hot. "Flaps 15," Frank yelled.

Tate moved the flap level. Nothing happened. "Flaps inop," Tate quickly warned.

Frank nodded. Had the fog thickened and dropped lower?

Suddenly Tate yelled. "I see the approach lights."

"Gear," Frank ordered.

The copilot quickly pushed the lever down. "Gear handle down." He glanced at the instrument panel again and his face muscles tightened.

"Starboard and nose gears not down and locked," Tate shouted.

Frank quickly glanced at the gear panel indicators. "Gear up. Tell the attendants to assume crash position. Can't go around."

"Roger." Tate pulled the lever up and spoke the warning instructions into the cabin microphone which probably nobody could hear. But the attendants could tell that the touchdown was near and showed the passengers that they should fold their arms on their knees and bend forward.

Frank brought back the power lever and raised the aircraft nose slightly.

This gave the appearance of the fast moving aircraft floating just above the ground. When the aircraft nose rose and the airspeed slowed, the whole plane shuddered and a wing dipped dangerously close to touching the ground but was quickly leveled by Frank as he plopped the airliner down on the runway. It skidded on its belly in excess of one hundred fifty miles an hour. Sliding, the airliner fuselage scraped along the top of the asphalt runway sounding like fingernails grating across a blackboard magnified a thousand times. Sparks from the friction erupted under the airliner making it look like a giant sparkler.

It was now out of Frank's control and he and the crew and passengers sweated out the seemingly endless minute as the aircraft slowly turned sideways before grinding to a stop.

Emergency vehicles, lights flashing, quickly surrounded the fuselage. Firemen shot foam into the smoking starboard engine as passengers evacuated their aluminum tube by sliding down emergency chutes. Surprisingly, a few of them appeared hardly fazed by their ordeal. Others, shaking, sobbed tears of joy, just happy to be on the ground in one piece. An elderly couple, traumatized and pale, was put into an ambulance.

Frank and the copilot jumped down to the runway from the food service door aft of the cockpit. They walked a short distance, then turned and looked back.

Now that it was over, Frank started to fully realize the implication of what could've happened and he suddenly felt exhausted. The pilots, deep in their own thoughts, remained silent for several seconds, gazing blankly at the remains of the airliner.

Tate broke the silence first. "My ears hurt."

"Mine, too."

"As they say, any landing you can walk away from is a good landing. Cool touchdown, Captain."

"Thanks. But when the company sees their aircraft, they're going to question that."

"Hah, as if those desk nerds could do better," Tate said.

Frank smiled and gripped the copilot on the shoulder. "Couldn't have done without you, good job." His voice then cracked. "We lost Beth."

Tate nodded silently.

Frank turned and headed toward a side door in the terminal. "See you later. I'm going to catch a hop back to Austin after I complete about a thousand pounds of paperwork."

It was midnight at the Austin–Bergstrom International Airport when Frank, still in his WestSky uniform and carrying his flight briefcase, exited with other passengers through the arrival gate. Nicole Braden, Frank's wife, a slender small-breasted woman in her mid-40s, ran out from a group of onlookers into his arms and held him tightly.

The walked down the terminal passageway arm-in-arm. "Nice going. Were you afraid?" She said.

"Too busy to get scared." A frown crossed his face. "Almost lost it. Don't know how it stayed together."

"TV anchors elevated you from a mere mortal into a Greek God."

"Couldn't have done it without my crew." Frank shook his head. "Our lead flight attendant, Beth, was sucked out the hole."

"Oh my God, that's terrible." Nicole's face turned chalky white. "The newscasts hinted about a casualty but they didn't have any details."

"I phoned her family. I guess I should've allowed the company to do that but they drag their feet about things like that. I felt I owed that to her. That was the toughest thing I had to do tonight." Frank stopped her in the middle of the terminal walkway and hugged Nicole again.

Their English Tudor style home sat just off Lake Austin, amid a scattering of upper middle class homes on the hilly shoreline terrain.

Frank followed Nicole through the doorway, stopped and looked around. "Where's Badger?"

"She must've wandered off again. I've been looking in the neighborhood for her all day. Nobody's seen her."

She hasn't done that in a long time, Frank thought. He really missed her leaping, friendly greeting he got every time he entered the house. "I guess she'll come home when she gets hungry." Frank sat down in an easy chair, twirled his cap through the air onto the sofa, and yawned. Nicole went into the kitchen and returned. She handed him a cup of coffee.

"I phoned Susan and Richard in their dorms to let them know their dad's okay," Nicole said as she sat down, looking proudly at her husband on the couch.

Frank sighed as he acknowledged her warm admiration. I guess she'll stick around for a while. Nothing like a near death experience to rekindle the passion, he told himself.

Frank yawned. "God. It's been a long day."

"Do they know what happened to your plane?"

"Metal fatigue is my guess. It ripped away in the slipstream and left a large hole underneath the first class compartment."

"Oh, my God," Nicole gasped.

"The FBI started questioning passengers as I left last night. I'm going to meet with them next week in Washington." Frank tried to stifle a yawn but failed. "I'm also temporarily grounded until the company completes their investigation, too. That's standard procedure." He handed Nicole his cup and she took it into the kitchen. When she returned, Frank was asleep.

2

The black wall of the Vietnam War Memorial in Washington D.C. sank beneath the ground level like a grave. Frank stood among a wide variety of tourists gazing or reaching out to copy indentations of names on the wall. Some were dressed in the standard tourist fare. Others wore portions of jungle fatigues, either tops or bottoms, and green combat jungle boots, courtesy of their old military units or deceased relatives.

Frank's eyes were moist as he touched the indentation of 'Jack Braden.' "I didn't mean it, Jack," he said softly.

Later that morning, Frank entered the FBI Headquarters building and was directed to a conference room by a uniformed man at the information desk. Inside the room, several agents and an airline executive sat around a long, rectangular metal table. When Frank entered the room, FBI Agent Tim Coffey, 50, a nervous man of medium height with a disarming smile, rose and offered his hand. He looked directly into Frank's eyes. "Good morning, Captain Braden. I'm Agent Coffey in charge of this investigation. Did your wife fly up with you?"

"Couldn't make it. You know how busy surgeons are."

"Everything okay at home?" Coffey asked.

"Yes. Why?"

"Oh, nothing, just part of our procedure."

Frank took a seat and folded his hands on top of the table. He noticed that an airline executive from West Sky was at the meeting and Frank nodded to him. The executive, sitting at the far end of the table, did not acknowledge the greeting. Frank thought that was strange since he once had been introduced to the man.

A minute of silence passed before Coffey, studying some papers in front of him, looked up at Frank. "I see you visited the Vietnam Memorial before you came over here."

"How'd you know?"

"Part of our procedures. Lose a buddy over there?"

"My older brother."

"Was he a pilot, too?" Coffey asked.

Frank shook his head. "No. He was a warrant officer with the Army CID. He got nailed by the guys he investigated in 'Nam."

"They ever catch 'em?" Coffey appeared impatient.

Frank shifted uncomfortably in his seat and looked at his watch. "They, uh, died over there, too."

"Interesting." Coffey made some hurried notes on his writing pad and looked up with a serious expression. "Okay, let's get to the point. A bomb went off in the luggage compartment. Of course, you knew that, right?"

"Jesus!" Frank bolted upright in his chair. "I assumed it was metal fatigue. Nothing written about a bomb in the newspapers."

"We delayed our findings to the news media until we were more positive."

"How did it get by security?" Frank was breathing faster now. *We were closer to eternity than I figured.*

The agent scratched the back of his neck and rose from his chair. "The way the bomb got aboard your

31

aircraft was unique." Coffey walked around the table and stopped behind him. Frank, uncomfortable that someone was standing close behind him, turned around.

Coffey leaned toward Frank. "It will save us all a lot of grief and time if you tell us now. Did you intend to commit suicide?"

Frank looked at Coffey as if he couldn't believe what the agent just said. "Excuse me?"

The agent leaned back as he studied Frank. He obviously enjoyed this game of cat and mouse. He silently paced the length of the table. His next question came in a nonchalant manner. "Do you have a dog?"

"No, no, what you said before," Frank said, somewhat dumbfounded.

"We'll get back to that. Do you own a dog?" Coffey said in a louder voice.

"Yes, or we did until a few days ago. Our Lab is missing."

The FBI agent strutted back to his paperwork and momentarily shuffled through them. He again looked up at Frank. "In your teens you had some experience with taxidermy. Correct?"

Frank looked questioningly at the agent. "I really don't see where—"

"Please answer the question."

"Yes, sir, it was a hobby."

"A small package of explosive material was sewn into the belly of a Lab," the agent said softly before pointing his finger and proclaiming in a louder voice. "Your dog, Mister Braden. That's how you got it aboard your aircraft." Coffey placed his hands on his hips and waited silently for Frank's reaction.

For a moment Frank felt as if he had fallen through the looking glass and was staring into the face of a

Cheshire cat. He had come to Washington expecting to use his expert knowledge of airline flying to help the FBI understand the metal fatigue problem that nearly killed himself, his passengers and crew aboard the aircraft he commanded. Suddenly, he was the accused. He also noticed that he was no longer referred to as Captain but as Mister Braden.

"The bomb residue was all over what was left of Fido and the kennel," Coffey added.

Frank composed himself and demanded, "Are you sure?"

"The baggage handler remembers putting the kennel on board. He stated that the dog appeared to be asleep. Figured it was sedated. He remembered the name on the shipping tag."

"What was the name?"

"Yours."

Frank leaped out of his seat. Three agents simultaneously rose quickly out of their seats. Coffey motioned them to sit back down. He turned to Frank. "Please sit down."

Frank, his heart racing, complied and returned to his seat.

"That's crazy. If I intended to bring a bomb aboard, why in hell would I be dumb enough to use my name on the shipping tag."

Coffey smiled. "That's simple. You didn't expect you and the plane to return."

"But it did and I brought it safely down. If I had wanted to kill myself without detection, I could've easily done it then."

"Ah, but then you had a copilot who could have stopped you or at least radioed your errant behavior to the ground," Coffey said. "Or you could have had a change of heart."

"Why would I do something like that, anyway?" Frank demanded.

Coffey calmly returned to his questioning. "We've been going over your history."

"So?"

"Your father committed suicide, didn't he?"

Frank glanced at the airline executive. The man took out a notebook and wrote in it. That was one piece of information that he failed to mention on his original airline application. "That was never proven," Frank said quickly. "The coroner's report stated that the cause of death was inconclusive."

"Then why did the insurance company contest it in court?"

"It was a big policy, I guess."

"Didn't your father take some considerable losses in the stock market just prior to his death. And didn't that insurance money keep your mother, sister and brothers from being destitute?" Coffey nodded his head as he spoke with sympathy in his voice, attempting to get Frank to agree.

"How would I know? I was barely five," Frank said calmly.

Coffey walked away, somewhat frustrated with Frank's resistance to his tactics. He figured he had a mentally unstable human before him and he wasn't going to let him escape responsibility for his actions. My God, this man not only tried to kill himself to give his family money and to cover it up for the insurance payoff, he tried to sacrifice a hundred and ten other people who had trusted their lives to him. Coffey turned around with a more aggressive attitude and put his face almost into Frank's face.

"Didn't you have some recent stock losses?" Coffey said loudly.

Frank noticed the airline executive taking notes again. He felt his blood pressure rising as he looked into Coffey's face only inches away. He tried to keep his cool and quickly answered, "Some."

"SOME," Coffey yelled, backing away from Frank and picking up some papers from the table. After he looked at them he waved the papers at Frank. "I would say 1.2 million dollars is quite 'SOME.' How MUCH do you have in your bank account right now?"

"That's my business."

"Oh, no," corrected Coffey. "That's our business. Need I remind you that we're conducting an investigation of a bombing of a national airliner and you're required to answer our questions. You know I can summon federal marshals to conduct you to a holding cell down the hall."

Frank realized Coffee was right and changed his attitude.

"Well, after we paid off some of our debt, I'd say a couple thousand."

"Couple thousand, eh. That's not very much for the neighborhood you live in, is it?"

"We'll get by."

"Sure about that? Don't you have two kids in a fairly expensive private college? TCU, I believe."

"Look, I'm a senior airline captain making nearly $145,000 a year and my wife is a noted surgeon, making twice that."

Coffey, moving in for the kill, held some paperwork in front of Frank. "If you're so well off why did you file Chapter 11 bankruptcy proceedings just prior to your near fatal flight?"

"To pay off the remainder of our debt over a due course of time, or don't you know the difference between a Chapter Eleven and a Chapter Seven?"

Coffey glared at Frank and went back to his table and picked up more paperwork. He now knew that he had underestimated his prey and that Frank would walk, at least for today. "Your military record is spotless except for one major incident."

"Yes sir."

"You killed an American officer in Vietnam."

"That was self defense, sir."

"We'll check it out," Coffey said.

"Be my guest."

The last remark caused Coffey to lose his composure. "Look, by the time we get through examining your past, we'll know every time you scratched your butt. Understand? I'm giving you one last chance to make it easy on yourself. Are you responsible for the bomb aboard WestSky Flight two-five-three?"

Frank, his blood again rising, snapped the pencil he was holding in half. "Not only no, but hell no. Don't you know that a terrorist is still out there while you're wasting your time with me? Man, have you lost your reasoning?" Frank stood up and put his face right in Coffey's face. "Are you through or do I call my attorney?"

Coffey jabbed his pointed finger into Frank's chest. "That's all for now. We'll contact you later. In the meantime, don't try to leave the country."

Frank moved straight toward the door and right through an unyielding Coffey. Their shoulders bumped hard. There were no apologies. Coffey made a threatening move toward Frank but was restrained by another agent.

3

Later that evening, Frank rammed his shoulder into the heavy boxing bag after delivering a thundering left hook into its center. He then exploded with a fury of lefts and rights into the bag. He had set up the bag in the garage as one form of exercise and to expend any frustrations accumulated during the day after a particularly aggravating flight. The bag came in very handy after returning from Washington. He stopped when the garage door rose and a GMC Suburban drove in with Nicole behind the wheel.

"Hey, champ. How did things go in Washington?" Nicole said leaning out the window.

Frank turned and nodded. He always felt embarrassed when Nicole saw him working out with the punching bag. He knew that Nicole considered him a gentle person who went out of his way to avoid conflict. He held out his arms for Nicole to pull off the bag gloves.

"Wow, the way you were hitting that bag, I hope you weren't thinking of me."

"Now you know," Frank said sheepishly. "Just getting rid of tension."

Nicole grinned. "I got a better way for you to do that."

Frank, sweat trickling down his forehead, leaned against the wall. He looked at Nicole's slender body and figured that wasn't a bad idea after a shower. For the first time that day, he smiled.

"I'm getting nervous. What happened in Washington? Do they know anything? It wasn't a bomb was it?" Nicole said excitedly.

"Yes, it was a bomb. Worse, it got aboard my aircraft in the belly of a Lab."

"You mean like Badger?"

"I mean Badger."

Nicole dropped her purse and stared at Frank. "You're kidding. Say you're kidding." She looked into Frank's eyes. "You're not kidding. Oh God, poor Badger. How? Why? Who would do such a thing?" She felt dazed. "I've got to go in and sit down." She picked her purse and stepped into the doorway and turned around. "What does this mean?"

"It means I went from superman to super suspect. It means that someone tried to implicate me in his crime. The shipping label for the dog carrier was in my name. The head jerk in charge of the FBI investigation thinks I tried to commit suicide."

Nicole leaned against the doorframe. "Tell me this is a bad dream."

"WestSky put me on permanent suspension pending the outcome of the investigation."

"You, attempt to commit suicide? For what reason?"

"Our market losses, the fact that we are nearly bankrupt. And because of my father. . . ."

Nicole, in a daze, started to walk into the kitchen, stopped and turned. "You didn't, did you?"

Frank quickly looked up with hurt in his eyes. But Nicole had already fled into the kitchen. He started to follow Nicole through the door, stopped, and angrily used his bare fist to smack the upper portion of the bag that he visualized as Coffey's face. He quickly walked by a bewildered Nicole sitting at the breakfast table. The thought of a romantic interlude that evening had completely vanished from his mind. He noticed tears in her eyes. After her last remark, he wondered whether they were for Badger or for him.

"Tomorrow I'm meeting in Dallas with representatives from the pilot's union. I going to fight this," he said tersely. He proceeded into their living room and went upstairs to the bedroom.

Nicole sat at the table wiping away her tears. She felt terrible about being skeptical and didn't blame him for his burst of anger toward her. At the moment she didn't understand herself, doubting him when he needed her. But why was the FBI so sure he had planted the bomb? And why would a terrorist frame him? He had never acted strange after losing all that money, she reasoned. And that was as much her fault as it was his. She had approved of his ventures in the stock market knowing that there were risks.

And wasn't he the same moral man, and a good lover and father to boot, she had fallen in love with twenty-one years earlier? Only time would tell if he was falsely accused. Either way she was determined to give him love and support during this ordeal and, God forgive, to get him medical help if needed. She went upstairs to make amends and to start that support.

In the pre-dawn darkness of the next morning, a figure, wearing dark coveralls, quietly approached the side window of Frank's garage. Noiselessly, he pulled out a screwdriver and quickly and silently pried open the window and climbed inside. He walked by the large GMC Suburban Wagon and opened the hood. He reached in and unhooked the battery connector cable. He then went to a smaller red sedan. He opened the rear door and knelt on the floor out of the sight of the driver's view. Thirty minutes later, he heard the garage door open and reached in a side pocket and pulled out a sealed plastic bag containing a rag.

Frank climbed in his red Acura and pulled out of their garage. He stopped in the driveway by their front porch and rolled down the tinted car window. He looked at a sharply dressed Nicole who was standing on the front porch holding a cup of coffee in her hand and a worried frown on her face.

"Hey, stop worrying. Everything's going to turn out okay. Good luck with your surgery this morning," Frank said.

Nicole relaxed and lost her frown. "You got it all wrong. You should wish my patient luck. I'll be behind you. I'm leaving in about ten minutes."

The homes in the area were about an eighth of a mile apart tied together by an isolated, tree-lined private road leading to a highway a mile away. A gated railroad crossing sat a half-mile ahead. Frank was driving at a careful speed, watching for deer that might suddenly appear in his headlights, when he heard a thump in the rear of his auto. Thinking he might have struck an animal, he pulled over to the side of the road and stopped. He reached for the door handle just as a dark figure rose up from the back seat and put a well-muscled forearm around his neck and pulled him tight against the back of his seat.

"What the . . .," Frank said. He tried to pry the arm off but was unsuccessful. Still struggling to breathe, he felt a wet, smelly cloth pressed over his mouth and nose. And that was the last thing he remembered.

Several minutes later, Nicole climbed into her Suburban and turned the ignition on several times. Nothing. Instead of going inside and phoning AAA or some other service, she opened the hood and spotted the disconnected battery cable. She figured it must have come loose after her last drive. Nicole was no dummy about mechanics. Her father had operated the largest car repair shop in their hometown and she had learned a lot about engines. She reconnected the cable in a jiffy.

Nicole, driving along same road that Frank had driven a few minutes earlier, was enjoying a rendition of Beethoven's Fifth Symphony over the radio when she was startled to see a stalled vehicle in the middle of the railroad tracks ahead of her. The vehicle sat between the two lowered railway gates. Red lights were flashing, bells were ringing and a train's horn was blaring as the Amtrak's bright light illuminated the sedan.

Nicole's eyes grew wide as she drew closer and recognized Frank's Acura. A figure sitting in the stalled car's driver seat was not moving. Without hesitation, Nicole blew her horn and stomped on the accelerator. The big Suburban, equipped with a large steel bumper guard, crashed through the barrier gates and pushed the stalled vehicle forward right through the second barrier gate to safety. Nicole then slammed the Suburban into reverse and backed out of harm's way seconds before the train, brakes shrieking and sparks flying, skidded past.

4

Frank opened his eyes and thought he saw a fuzzy image of Nicole standing over him. He rolled his head from side to side and slowly Nicole and the white room came into focus. "Where," he said slowly, "am I?"

"Emergency room at Seton."

"How long have I been out?"

"An hour. How are you feeling?"

Frank smiled weakly. "Like I attended one hell of a party." He tried to rise but fell back on the pillow holding his head. "Boy, I could use some aspirins."

"I'll tell the nurse. Are you still woozy?"

"A little out of focus, but improving," Frank replied. "But you're the doctor. What's your diagnosis?"

Nicole took his hand gently. "For starters, you could be accused of falling asleep on the tracks or simply trying to destroy yourself and maybe an Amtrak train to boot."

"Wow. I guess the guy who put me out had serious intentions."

Nicole rubbed her hand tenderly through his hair. She started to say something then paused and rethought her approach. "Frank, I found you unconscious, alone at the wheel, in front of a very noisy Amtrak."

42

"How did I get out of that one?"

"I bumped you across the tracks."

"Good thing I married you." Frank gave her a weak smile. "Nobody else in the car?"

"As they say, only in your dreams." Nicole, looking distraught, pondered her next question before speaking. "Did you take anything between our house and the railroad tracks?"

Frank, now a little more alert, looked puzzled at her question. "Take anything? You mean like a drug?"

"Yes, medicine, you know, anything, the doctors here need to know."

"You mean, you need to know," Frank said tersely.

"Frank, I didn't mean. . . ."

"Look, I'm telling you the truth. Someone hid in the back seat and put a rag, probably soaked in chloroform, over my face shortly after I left the house."

Nicole tried to keep disbelief from her face, but failed. Tears burst forth from her eyes. Frank changed his demeanor and beckoned her to him. She bent over and he hugged her tight. "I need you now more than ever to believe me. I know that everything seems to point to me but accept what I say as true. Someone is deliberately stalking me. He now has tried to kill me twice. I don't who or why but he's apparently trying to make it look like a suicide and he doesn't care how many lives he may have to destroy to do it."

"Darling, I want to believe you."

"Understand this. No way do I want to intentionally leave you and the kids because of some stupid insurance money."

"Besides, remember if I die, it'll be probably be by drowning, not suicide," Frank said, trying to be jovial.

"That's not funny, either," Nicole rebuked.

Frank had to agree with that. He still had a fear of deep water ever since he had almost drowned in a river when he was seven. He was with a friend at the time. The friend drowned while Frank was pulled from the depths where he also had been tangled in the undergrowth. As a result, Frank developed a mild form of aquaphobia and would never swim in anything outside of a swimming pool.

Nicole, frightened and confused, held Frank tighter. "I'm calling the police."

"No, for God's sake. It'll look like I tried to commit suicide again. If you didn't believe me at first, what do you think the FBI would think? That could really kiss my career goodbye."

Nicole slowly nodded her head in agreement. "This is scary. Why on earth would somebody try to kill you?"

"Beats me," Frank said as he slowly got out of bed and started to dress himself. "By the way, what happened to your patient this morning?"

"I had Doctor Murphy take over for me. He owed me one. Let's go home."

Late that night as Nicole climbed into bed with her already sleeping husband, she lay there for an hour unable to sleep. During that hour, many conflicting thoughts crossed her mind.

Did someone plant a bomb aboard the airliner using our dog as the carrier? Frank was unconscious when I found him in the car. Who to believe, the FBI or Frank? Or could Frank be a latent schizophrenic, believing that a phantom stalker was responsible while he was doing it himself all along? Schizophrenia, she knew from her medical background, is an inherited trait, a bad gene, so to speak.

Nicole climbed out of bed and went into the bathroom for water. Staring into the cabinet mirror, she continued her restless and disturbing thoughts.

Schizophrenics have a high suicide rate. And Frank's father was suspected of committing suicide. But Frank's brothers and sisters have never shown signs of the trait. And the symptoms usually occur in more than one sibling and make its appearance between the ages of seventeen to twenty-two.

No, she smiled. *It's not schizophrenia, thank God. I must believe Frank, for our love and for my own sanity.* Now exhausted, Nicole went back to bed and fell into a deep sleep.

The next morning Frank came down the stairs wearing a beige cardigan sweater. He gave Nicole a tight good morning hug at the breakfast table. "Off to the hospital this morning?" Frank questioned.

Nicole nodded. "Maybe I shouldn't leave. Doctor Murphy can do the operation for me." She looked at him questioningly.

"Hey, I'm not a cripple. I can take care of myself."

"I'm putting in for a vacation. We'll go somewhere until this all blows over." Nicole said.

Frank shook his head. "If this guy is out to get me, I don't want you around."

"What are we going to do?"

"There must be some answers to all of this."

"I think we should still call the police."

"No." Frank was adamant. "I'm going to sit down and think this out, even if it takes me all week."

Nicole picked up her purse. "I'm coming right back after the operation. Promise me you won't leave the house. He may be out there, waiting."

"I won't even go into the yard."

Nicole gave him another hug and recoiled when her hand felt a hard object in the small of his back. ""What's that?"

Frank shrugged. "A snub nose .38."

"Why?"

"Jesus, I'm not going to shoot myself. But whoever is trying to do me in is dangerous." Frank saw the worried stare in Nicole's eyes. "You got to trust me." He turned away from her. "Look, I'll cancel the insurance policy on me if that's want you want. Then I'd have no reason to kill myself."

Sensing his anger, Nicole felt like kicking herself. *I will believe him.* "No don't do that, I'll need the money," she managed to say with a humorous demeanor.

Frank turned and smiled for the first time that morning. "Believe me, we'll find that nutcase, right?"

Nicole put on her best brave face and slowly walked out of the door, looking back several times.

"Don't worry, I won't even leave the house." Five minutes later, Frank left the house and got into his red Acura. He hated lying to Nicole but figured the fastest way to find this stalker was to make the bait visible. Only this time he looked behind the front seat before he drove off.

After reaching Route 71, a four-lane highway, Frank, driving in the curb lane, headed toward the Austin-Bergstrom International Airport. He drove slower than normal, occasionally glancing at the rearview mirror. Nothing back there, he noted. Just two minivans of moms and children and a taxicab tailed him. Other trucks and cars passed him at a high rate of speed. Perhaps the guy thought the train got me and hasn't found out yet. Maybe I get a day or two of reprieve, Frank reasoned.

"That's one lucky sucker," the driver thought, as he drove the stolen green and yellow cab behind Frank. If the word got around that he missed twice, it might hurt his reputation. And respect meant everything to him. He had been successful on scoring on his victims always on the first attempt, until now. Several years ago, he had spent three years in prison for armed robbery before turning to the art of killing people for money. All he had gotten out of the robbery of that liquor store was a lousy three hundred dollars or about a hundred dollars for each year in jail. He found that being an assassin was much more lucrative to support his drug habit and actually was safer than armed robbery because the majority of victims rarely knew their life was in danger. Hurting other people had never been a problem to him.

After reaching the airport, Frank pulled in the private parking lot marked for employees of WestSky Airlines. The taxicab behind him continued toward the main terminal. Before exiting his car, Frank placed his revolver in the glove compartment. He walked toward WestSky's Airline Dispatcher's office and entered. He saw the chief dispatcher, Charley Love, at his desk and walked over. Charley, a black man in his fifties, looked up and smiled when he saw Frank.

47

"When are you coming back?" Charley stood up and they shook hands.

"Don't know. Trying to find out how that bomb got aboard my aircraft. Were you on duty that day?" Frank said.

"Sure was. Can't forget that day after I heard what you went through."

"Anything unusual happen before my flight took off that night."

Charley scratched his head and shook his head, no. "Nope, just normal, I guess."

Frank looked disappointed but pressed on. "Maybe an unusual phone call or something?"

Charley's eyes brightened. "Now you mentioned it, there was a call for you but on the day before your flight. The guy wanted to know if you would be stopping by the next evening at his place. I just told him I didn't think so because you were scheduled for a flight on the night Washington run. He didn't leave a message and said he would call you at home."

Frank looked at Charley questioningly. "Did he say who he was?"

"I believe a restaurant manager, uh, at Green Acres. He wanted to complete arrangements for your anniversary party."

"Did he give a name?" Frank quickly asked.

"Didn't think to ask. I figured you knew."

"Can you recall anything about his voice, you know, the manner in which he spoke?"

"Sure, that's easy," Charley said, "high pitched, almost feminine—." Charley, sensing that something was amiss, paused. "What's wrong?"

"My anniversary's not 'till next August."

48

"Oh, I'm sorry. I better phone that local FBI agent and tell him about the call."

Frank only nodded though he could hardly contain his excitement. Here was the first proof that another person was involved.

5

Frank drove away from the airport and relaxed when he saw only a green and yellow taxicab behind him. His exhilaration had faded during the walk to his car. What now, he had asked himself? It was still up to the unknown stalker to make a move when and where he wanted to strike. At least the FBI would be alerted that a phony phone call had inquired about him and his flight the day before. Oh, well, it's a start. Just maybe that wiseass Coffey might get a hint that there's an unknown assassin out there.

Now there was a lot of traffic behind him on Route 71 and Frank decided to make sure he wasn't being tailed. He figured he'd do what he saw in the movies. He turned right onto Riverside Drive heading west until he reached Congress Avenue. Then he turned north on Congress, crossed Town Lake and headed into the downtown area. Watching his rearview mirror, he turned left onto Sixth Street and a block later made another left and then turned left again onto Fifth Street. He sped up and went one block and made a quick right turn onto Congress Avenue again, heading south.

He looked into his rearview mirror and saw only a bus and three taxicabs behind him, two Yellow Cabs and a green and white one. That confirmed to him that the stalker didn't know he wasn't dead yet. He felt a tinge of disappointment. Then feared gripped him. What if the guy was waiting for him inside his house? What if Nicole arrived home before him? He pulled out his cell phone and dialed Seton Hospital. He felt relieved when the hospital staff told him that Nicole was still in surgery and wasn't expected to leave the hospital before early afternoon.

Frank decided to give the stalker one more chance. After stopping off at a store where he bought a donut and a cup of coffee, he headed west on Riverside Drive to Zilker Park. Inside the park, Frank selected an isolated parking lot near the soccer fields. He reached into his glove compartment and put his revolver in a pocket of his cardigan sweater, exited the car and walked to a nearby park table. Sitting on the table edge facing the road, he sipped his coffee. He had an excellent view of any car that would come his way. Behind him was the wide-open meadow of a soccer field.

Five minutes later, Frank's body tightened. A black sedan with a male driver, cruised slowly past, then stopped and backed up. The driver smiled at him through an open window. That's when Frank realized it was a man looking for intimate male companionship. Frank quickly looked away, and the driver, looking disappointed, sped off.

A green and white cab pulled into a parking lot a hundred yards behind Frank on the other side of the soccer field. The driver, wearing a business suit, climbed out and silently moved toward his target like a lion stalking prey, keeping himself out of sight by aligning with Frank's back. In a minute he was within lethal shooting range of Frank.

Frank's attention was again drawn to another car in the distance that was coming down the same road, only a little faster this time. When the car drove past without slowing, Frank again felt let down from the anticipation he was experiencing.

"That car was going a little too fast for this road, Mister Braden. Wouldn't you agree?" The man was pleased that he was able to get within range of yet another prey undetected. He loved it once his victims were securely within his grasp. He spoke in a pleasant, high-pitched voice that had a victorious ring to it.

Frank's heart practically jumped into his throat as he heard the nearly feminine accent behind him. He whirled to face its owner and saw a pockmarked smiling face belonging to a large man in his middle thirties. Since Frank feared the worst, the man's smile confused him.

"Didn't hear you come up."

"Part of my trade." The man grinned and flashed a FBI badge. "I got orders to bring you in."

"I'd like to see some other identification, please," Frank said.

The man nodded and pulled a 9mm pistol from a shoulder holster inside his jacket and pointed it at Frank.

Frank tried to look calm. "Hey, I'm a respectable airline captain with a big mortgage, a wife and two kids in college. You don't really need a gun to escort me to your headquarters building, do you?" As Frank spoke he nonchalantly placed his hands in the pockets of his cardigan sweater. His right fingers carefully wrapped around the revolver and he pointed it inside the pocket at the supposed agent. Now Frank felt a little more secure.

"Sorry, sir, that's my orders." The man shrugged his shoulders and genuinely looked apologetic that he had to carry out his duty that way. He reached onto his belt and brought out a pair of handcuffs. "I'm afraid that you'll have to wear these, too, sir," he said politely.

"By the way, how are we going to get to your head-quarters?" Frank said, looking around.

The man nodded toward Frank's car.

"Wait a minute, how did you get here?"

"By taxi," he said honestly. He drew closer to Frank to put the cuffs on.

"I'm not going to put on those cuffs and you know why," Frank said, backing away.

The sudden determination in Frank's voice told the man that the game had ended. He looked at Frank with a cold stare. "My employer preferred that you have an accident or commit suicide. But too much time has elapsed."

"Who sent you?"

The man shook his head. "In my business, we rarely meet our employer. The man quickly looked around and then raised his pistol towards Frank's head.

Frank's finger tightened around his own revolver's trigger and he fired twice directly through his sweater into the man's chest. A surprised look appeared on the man's face as he gasped and fell backwards onto the ground.

Frank pulled out his revolver and bent down. He carefully felt the man's neck for a pulse. There wasn't any. Frank went back to his car, picked up a cell phone, paused, and sat it back down again. He returned to the body and searched through the man's clothing. The guy's wallet contained only the FBI identification card and cash. There was no driver's license to otherwise identify the man. But mixed in among nine hundred dollars was a small white slip that displayed the number 2310180920531335779. Frank thought that was odd and copied it. He then placed the slip back into the dead man's wallet.

He returned to his vehicle and pulled out a business card and dialed its number on his cell phone.

"Agent Coffey, please."

A minute passed before a familiar voice came on the phone. Frank involuntarily shuddered at the sound.

"Coffey here."

Frank was breathing hard now. "This is Frank Braden."

"I'll be dammed." There was a slight pause and Frank guessed that Coffey was waving his arms around madly, trying to get someone to tape the call. Within seconds, Coffey was back on the line. "Ready to bare your soul, flyboy?"

"I just shot the man who probably planted the bomb aboard my flight. I thought you ought to know before I call the police."

"Where are you?" Coffey sounded confused.

"In Austin. At Zilker Park, next to the soccer fields.

"Is the person you shot still alive?" Coffey said.

"Dead."

"Why do you think this is the guy who planted the bomb?"

"He posed as an FBI agent and tried to handcuff me."

"God," exploded Coffey. "You shot one of my agents, you idiot. I had sent one down there to keep an eye on you."

There was dead silence on both ends of the phone. The news sent a tremor throughout Frank's body before he composed himself. Slowly he brought the phone to his lips again. "Did you order him to handcuff me and bring me in?"

"I didn't but that doesn't make any difference. One of my directors could have ordered it without informing me."

"You don't understand. This guy had his gun pointed at me and admitted he was sent to kill me. Don't your agents carry credit cards, driver's license or other form of personal identification?"

"You mean this guy didn't?"

"He only had an FBI badge."

Frank could hear a sigh of relief from the phone. "Wasn't our agent, after all," Coffey said. "For that you can thank your lucky stars." There was another long pause before Coffey came back on line. "I just heard that our agent lost you in traffic. Something about you doing a lot of quick turns on Austin streets. Now stay where you are. I'm sending a car from our Austin office."

After disconnecting, Frank punched in three numbers on the cell phone. "Nine-one-one? Send an ambulance to the parking lot at Zilker soccer fields. A man has been shot."

While Frank leaned against the table waiting for the police, he looked at the long number that he had found in his assailant's pocket. It appeared to Frank as a serial number off a VCR or maybe a computer. He slipped the paper back into his pocket as a police car and ambulance arrived. A bureau car containing two men from the Austin office of the FBI arrived shortly after Frank completed a statement to the police. Frank was released to FBI custody after they spoke to the police officers. One of the FBI men stayed behind to examine the body and Frank followed the bureau vehicle in his car. Later, Frank was released to go home.

When he arrived, Nicole, who had been waiting for him, jumped off the couch.

"You told me you weren't going to leave the house."

"I'm sorry, honey. There was something I just had to do."

"There was something I almost had to do. Nicole held her index finger and thumb about an inch apart. "I was this far from calling the police." She started to cry. "I was afraid that they might find you in a ditch with a self-inflicted gunshot wound, damn you."

"Nicole, listen. It's all over." Frank moved forward and took his sobbing wife into his arms. "You don't have to worry about my harming myself, anymore. I found the stalker."

Nicole stopped crying and looked up. "How? Who? Where is he?"

"He's dead."

"Dead? How?"

"I shot him."

Nicole recoiled backward. "Are you in trouble?"

"Police seemed to agree that it was self defense. So does the FBI. His gun was in his hands."

"He tried to kill you. Why?"

"Paid to do it. But that's part of the problem. He claimed he didn't know who hired him." Frank plopped down on the couch and pulled a wide-eyed Nicole down with him.

Nicole grabbed Frank with both hands. "But it's not over, don't you see? This psycho can get another hired killer."

"Possible. But maybe he'll give up because I don't think he's a nutcase. He might be worried that the authorities are now alerted and could be closing in on him. The plan of getting the bomb aboard my airliner was almost too perfect," Frank said, rubbing his forehead. "This guy's clever."

Can't the FBI track him down through the dead person?" Nicole asked.

"I don't think so. The guy had only a false ID card on him with a fake name. I went through his pockets pretty good and found nothing but lots of cash and some serial number."

Frank pulled out the slip of paper and showed it to Nicole. She looked at it. "Perhaps, a serial number from a VCR set or something similar," she said.

"Maybe," Frank said, and started to put it back into his pocket but Nicole stopped him.

"Let me work it on the computer and see if it's more than a serial number." A gleam came into Nicole's eyes as she looked again at the numbers and went into their study. A few minutes later she emerged, smiling. "I think I may have gotten part of it."

She showed Frank a notepad on which she had written 205-313-5779. "These last ten digits fit perfectly into a phone number," she said. "That leaves 23101809 and I have no idea about them."

Frank grabbed the notepad. "Let me see those numbers." He stared hard at the digits. "Hmm. If you look at them with a military mind, they could equate to a time and date. The 2310 could mean ten minutes after eleven p.m. and 1809 would be September 18. So that would mean he was to call that number on that date. But if our guess is correct and since that date is over a month old, why would he still carry it in his wallet?"

"Unless he wanted to keep the telephone number," Nicole said.

"Maybe, but somehow, I doubt that. If he really didn't know who hired him, that phone number probably belongs to a phone in a public telephone booth and then it wouldn't be worth a plug nickel after that date."

"Okay, Sherlock," Nicole eagerly responded. "But doesn't the date normally come before the time in the military?" Nicole asked.

"But there isn't a twenty-third month." Frank suddenly sat up straight. "Except that the military always writes the day before the month instead of the civilian way of writing the day after the month." He then wrote down 23 October and nine minutes after six p.m.

"That's today," exclaimed Nicole.

Frank looked at his watch. "I've got six minutes after six." He took the notepad and went to the phone. Nicole rushed over to him and gave him her cell phone.

"Use this. It may not be a pay phone and he will be able to see who's calling if he has caller ID."

Frank took the cell phone and looked at his watch. It was exactly nine minutes after six. He dialed the number on the pad. The phone rang four times before a voice answered, "Is the mission accomplished?"

Frank threw a handkerchief over the mouthpiece. He didn't know whether that worked but he saw it used in the movies a lot, so he thought, what the heck. He then used his first imitation of a high-pitched voice and answered, "Yeah."

"No big news stink, right?"

"Yeah," Frank replied again.

"Accident or suicide?"

"Before I get into details, I want more money," Frank said.

"A deal's a deal."

"I'll tell you why I want more when I see you." Frank winked at Nicole who stood close to the phone, listening.

"I told you before, we'll never meet. Maybe I'll put a little more in your envelope." The phone went dead.

"Damn." Frank said. He looked at Nicole. "It's not over. That guy had such determination in his voice. I may be crazy but that voice also had a familiar ring to it. Anyway, we know the guy's in Washington. There shouldn't be any more attempts on my life at least for the next few days since the guy doesn't know I'm not dead yet. What I don't understand, though, is why there seems to be a timetable for my demise."

"Why do you say that?" Nicole paced the room.

"Before he died, the guy in the park said something to that effect. That he ran out of time to make my death look like a suicide or accident."

"Who do you know that would profit by your death by a certain time."

Nobody that's alive, Frank thought. He started to pace the room along with Nicole and stopped. "Naw." Frank said aloud. "It couldn't be. He's dead."

"Who."

"That voice." Frank looked at Nicole. "For a second, I thought it belonged to a dead man."

"Who," Nicole pleaded. "You're driving me crazy. Who?"

"A murdering, drug smuggling jerk by the name of Captain Miles Fenton. He's responsible for my brother's death in Vietnam."

"Could he be alive?"

"No. In fact, he got himself off easy by dying. The CIA was gathering enough evidence to give him a dishonorable discharge and put him in Leavenworth for ten lifetimes.

Nicole went into the kitchen and returned with a phone. "Here. Call the FBI back. At least they'll know that someone is trying to have you killed."

6

The next morning, Frank sat in the Austin office of the FBI. Agent Coffey, another agent and a stenographer also were present. Coffey, hands on his hips in a belligerent stance, towered over Frank.

"You mean I flew on a redeye flight to hear this 'Alice in Wonderland' tale?"

"Everything I told you is true," Frank said.

"Let's put this in perspective." The agent, bags under his eyes, sat down behind a desk while his fingers rubbed his chin. He stifled a yawn before he continued. "You're saying that someone in Washington hired an assassin to plant a bomb aboard an airliner just to kill you. He was willing to kill all those people just to kill you?"

"Yes sir. Probably to make it look like the suicide tale you swallowed. And when that failed he tried to have me killed twice more."

"Wait a minute. You mean once more, don't you?"

"We didn't tell you about the second attempt." Frank lowered his eyes. "Someone chloroformed me and left me in my car in front of an oncoming Amtrak. If it hadn't been for my wife who got me off the tracks, I would've been mixed in with smashed metal."

"Why weren't we informed?" Coffey said disbelievingly. "Do you have any evidence of this?"

"No. That's why we didn't report it. You'd think I tried to commit suicide again."

"Don't you think that'd be understandable on my part," Coffey said quietly.

"There was a knock on the door and Nicole entered. "I really think I should be in on this, if you don't mind."

Coffey did mind but he declined to deny her entry after seeing the determined look in her eyes. "Maybe you can shed some light on his fairy tale."

Nicole gave the agent a blistering look. "Did you run a check on the man my husband shot?"

"Yes ma'am. We don't know at this moment who he was. But we'll eventually find out."

"Great. My husband might be dead by that time," Nicole said.

Coffey winched. "Don't worry Mrs. Braden. If that man, indeed, was an assassin, we'll make every effort to protect your husband."

"What do you mean, *if* he was an assassin?"

Coffey saw his chance to get back on the offensive. "As far as we know, right now, he could have been just a robber. We only have your husband's word that the man identified himself as a hired killer."

"Did you trace the number that was on the body?" Nicole fired back.

"Yes, ma'am. It was a public pay phone in Washington."

"If you had made the initial call to that number instead of us, you might have taped it and got a voiceprint," Nicole bluntly pointed out. "What took you so long in deciphering that number? My God, a kid with a box top decoder ring could have broken it sooner."

Frank was amazed. He had never seen Nicole like this. She actually had Coffey squirming. He enjoyed it immensely.

Coffey coughed. He definitely wished she hadn't asked that particular question.

"Well, to be honest, at first, we thought it was just a serial number from a VCR set."

Frank and Nicole discreetly looked at each.

Coffey continued. "Once our analyst went over it later that night and discovered what it really was, the time to call had already passed. We tried but there was no answer." He walked over to the other agent and whispered to him. Coffey turned and came back to Nicole. "Please understand I am sympathetic to your plight, real or otherwise. But without evidence, there's little I can do at this point. However, since I'm authorized to put a tail on your husband, we can use the agent to keep an eye on your house, too. Although you have to realize that he has limited time and you won't be covered twenty-four hours a day." He looked directly at Frank. "For your sake, I hope that some of what you told me is true."

7

Late that same day a phone conversation took place in Washington.

"John, I need you on a very important job. It'll pay very well. You know me."

"Shoot."

"You have to catch a flight to Austin immediately. I need you on a disposal case."

"Got a name?"

"Yes. I'll fax you a photo with the necessary information tonight."

"Sounds like a rush job."

"John, it's very important that you get the job done within the next day or two and I don't care how you do it. Let me correct that. I'd like it to look like suicide but right now that isn't important as much as his immediate demise. Understand."

"Consider it done. But listen, it may be hard to book a flight immediately."

"Call me back right away if you have trouble and I'll get you a charter flight."

"Sounds like this target is a real threat to you."

"I'll not get into that but if you have to take out a member of his family along with him, let that not be a deterrent."

"Good, you just gave me a wide range of choices."

"I must warn you the guy is slippery. The last man I contracted this out to, supposedly with a good reputation in his field, died in the attempt. That's why I came to you."

"You know I never met a man I couldn't take out."

"Call me when it's over. You got my private number, right?"

"Sure do," John said. "But don't worry. I've never written it down."

8

It was nine at night, when the FBI agent watching Frank's house decided to drive down the road to get a cup of coffee. He figured it would take no longer than twenty minutes. Besides he was due to go off duty at midnight. It had been a long day for him, starting early in the morning, when Frank went out to jog along the deserted, curving two-lane road that ran in front of his house. He felt that this business of someone trying to assassinate the pilot sounded too much like paranoia. Besides, he had to report back here at six the next morning. He knew that this type of operation of following Frank and also watching his house, required a two-man shift and that he couldn't do it all by himself. He yawned and drove away, feeling that the assignment couldn't end soon enough.

As soon as the taillights of the agent's car disappeared down the road, a figure dressed in black coveralls, black sneakers and a black Navy watch cap stepped out of nearby bushes and walked quietly into Frank's dark, rear yard. He rubbed an itch on his black shaded nose with skintight black leather gloves as he circled the rear of the house. Through a window he could see Frank and a woman in a family room, having an animated

65

discussion. John was glad that the couple no longer had a dog. The fax sent by his employer had covered that detail. That made his job a lot simpler. When he arrived in Austin earlier that day, he really didn't have a plan. So he decided to look the situation over and make an on-the-job decision. He knew he could burst into the house immediately and gun them both down with a silencer and be out of the area in a minute. That would be simple, but too newsworthy, he thought. Besides, John always felt he had a conscience and hated to waste another life unless it was absolutely necessary. The fact that the woman he saw with Frank was gorgeous may have stirred that portion of his conscience. After all, a hit man has scruples, too. He should be paid for each victim, no two-for-one deal, he self-righteously thought.

Inside the family room, Nicole pleaded with Frank to hire a private detective to guard him. "It's only for a week or two and this will be all over."

"Don't you understand, we don't have the money in our budget to afford a personal guard. They are very costly and I'm not a movie or rock star." Frank had been adamant about that ever since Nicole brought it up earlier in the evening. "Hey, there's an FBI agent right outside our house now to protect us. What more do you want?"

"But he's only one man, Coffey said so himself. He can't stay here all night," Nicole pleaded.

"Look, let's not argue about this tonight. At least I should be safe for the next two days until our Washington friend finds out I'm not dead. In fact, he just may give it up, for whatever his reason for wanting me dead." Frank went over and sat down beside Nicole. "These attempts must've cost him a bundle and all he has accomplished so far is to alert the authorities that someone is trying to kill me and that I'm not really suicidal."

"Tell that to Coffey." Nicole reminded Frank. "He's still not sure about you."

"He'll come around." He gave Nicole a peck on the cheek and went over and turned on the television set and sat down in front of it. "Say, speaking of our agent, we never introduced ourselves. Why don't you go outside and offer him a cup of coffee. It wouldn't hurt to keep him happy."

"I got a better idea. I'll make the coffee and you take it to him," Nicole said.

A few minutes later, Frank went out the front door and looked for the agent's car. He didn't see any on the road. There were no streetlights and he peered into the darkness until his eyes adjusted to the light. That's when he saw an outline of a car parked off the road in some nearby bushes. Frank thought that was pretty sharp for the agent to keep out of sight. He started to cross the street when he heard a voice from the side of the yard.

"I'm back here."

Frank turned around and walked into the dark beside his house.

"Over here."

Frank thought the voice now came from the back yard and he continued toward the rear of the house. When he got to the rear yard, Frank still couldn't see the agent. "Hey, where in the devil are you? I got some hot coffee."

"I think I saw someone run into the foliage near the lake. You better go back inside where it's safe while I have a look around."

"No, I'll help you search. Wait a minute." Frank jogged towards the voice that seemed to be closer to the lake now.

Standing in the shadows, John smiled. For whatever reason, whether his victim was a macho know-it-all type or just naive of the danger, many of the men he had killed had swallowed that bait. He also figured from the fax sheet he had received, that the Austin police had taken Frank's .38-calber revolver. Under the new waiting law, John knew it was impossible for Frank to get another weapon so soon, unless his intended victim wasn't a law-biding citizen. And John was counting on Frank to be a law-abiding sort.

As Frank neared Town Lake, he wished he had brought a flashlight. He couldn't see the agent at all. So he went toward the shrubbery where he last heard the voice. "Hey, fellow, where are you?" Frank said. He felt foolish that he didn't know the agent's name.

"Here, right behind you."

The voice startled Frank and he whirled around to face a well-built man wearing all black as though he was on a Special Forces recon night team. I'm in trouble, Frank thought, as he looked down the silencer barrel of a 9mm pistol. God, this guy is really good. "Did you kill the agent that was watching me?"

"I wasn't paid to do that. Now, Frankie boy, let's me and you take a walk to the shoreline."

Frank ignored the order and stared at his assailant with a fierce determination. "Why should I? The water is a little chilly this time of the year."

"Because you'll live a little longer," John murmured, "not long, but most people regard those moments as precious."

Frank shrugged and acted like it was an offer he couldn't refuse. He turned and walked slowly to the lake with John staying close behind him. "I take it you're pretty good at this," Frank ventured, trying to get a conversation going.

"Hey, I was trained by the U.S. taxpayers. Ever hear of the Special Forces." John was having trouble seeing in the blackness. He knew that he needed glasses for improved night vision but had neglected to get a prescription. Now forty, he began to realize that he was mortal just like everybody else. Prior to this, he had always considered glasses a sign of physical inferiority. He liked to tout his macho image, his muscular build, and a full crop of black hair, especially around women, and glasses wouldn't hack it. I could use a flashlight, he thought, as he drew closer to Frank.

"All the Green Berets I knew were honorable men," Frank retorted.

"Not all," John said contritely. "So you were in the military, too?"

"Who sent you to do this?"

"You probably know him. He sure knows you."

Frank stopped at the water's edge, his back toward the killer. His mind raced rapidly on his next move. He knew the water was about 15-feet deep in this area and he considered diving in, hoping that his assailant might miss his shot because of the darkness. But then he hesitated, fearful of the deep, dark water

"You always murder fellow soldiers?"

"Yeah," John said nonchalantly. "I do my share." John thought about what he had just said and gave a low laugh. He raised the pistol high above Frank's head and grunted as he came down hard.

Frank, figuring his assailant's intentions and hearing the utterance, jerked his head to one side and the glancing blow caught Frank on the side, nearly rendering him unconscious. He fell into the water and disappeared beneath the surface.

John, unsure about the blow, cursed the darkness, and fired three times into the water where Frank had disappeared. He stood for two minutes waiting to see if his victim would surface. When he saw nothing, he felt satisfied that his mission had been accomplished, even though it might not be taken as a suicide if any of his bullets had struck home.

Frank, trying to keep from passing out from the blow, struggled underwater before he overcame his immobilizing fear of the depth, and, doing a version of the crawdad stroke, moved slowly beneath the surface parallel to the shoreline towards his neighbor's boat ramp. *Yes, you can make it. Think of it as a deep swimming pool.*

He hid under the ramp until he heard his assailant leave. Dragging himself onto shore, he staggered toward his house. In the distance, he saw the headlights of a car approaching.

When John saw the headlights, he pressed himself against the side of the house and waited.

Agent Philips parked in front of the house and turned off his headlights. Now having doubts about leaving his post for thirty minutes, he decided to knock on the door and introduce himself and make sure that nothing had happened while he was on the coffee run.

Nicole answered the doorbell with the smile of a welcome wagon hostess. "Hi, I'm Nicole. Did you like your coffee? I hope I didn't make it too strong."

The confusion on the agent's face told Nicole that something was wrong. That was confirmed seconds later when Frank stumbled in through the back door, dripping wet with blood running down the side of his head. Nicole screamed.

John used Nicole's scream as his cue for departure. He ran from the side of the house, across the street and to his car in the bushes. He started the car without turning on his headlights and pulled rapidly onto the road.

With the front door still open, Nicole, Philips and Frank heard the car pull away.

"That's the guy who just tried to kill me," Frank stammered. "Get me a wet towel, quick."

Nicole ran into the kitchen and gave the towel to Frank as he followed the agent outside. "We can't let him get away to strike again." Frank shouted at the agent.

Philips ran to his car and Frank followed, jumping into the passenger seat. He held the towel to his head as they sped down the curvy road hoping to draw near before the assailant reached the highway. Soon they saw the taillights of the fleeing car ahead. It was taking the curves at a dangerous speed, going off the shoulder of the road several times. Both cars went slightly into the air as they sped at high speed over the railroad tracks where Frank had nearly met his demise days earlier. "There's a nearly ninety degree turn to the right about a thousand feet ahead," Frank cautioned. "If he doesn't slow down he'll never make it."

In the car ahead, John realized that his trouble of seeing clearly at night was a major problem on that road at that speed. He had the accelerator to the floorboard but wasn't putting any distance between him and his pursuer. He wasn't sure who was in the car behind him but he thought about stopping around the next curve and taking them out. He glanced in the rear view mirror and never saw the acute right angle turn ahead. He tried to turn with the sharp curve at the last second but he was too fast and too late. The car's momentum rolled itself into a pair of big oak trees and came apart. The sudden impact broke his seat belt and hurled him against the collapsing metal structure of the vehicle that crushed itself against the unyielding base of the trees. The crash ended John's merciless career and the resulting flames consumed his body.

Both men in the pursuing car saw the crash ahead and slowed to a stop. They jumped out and ran toward the wrecked auto but the intense heat of the fire kept them at a distance. The agent called for help on his car phone and went back to stand by Frank.

"I think your troubles might be over now," the agent said while watching the fire consume the smashed auto.

"No way. Just before he tried to dump me in the lake, he told me that I probably know the man who hired him."

"I take it he didn't give you a name?"

Frank shook his head. Off in the distance they could hear sirens heading their way. "I was hoping that we could have taken him alive," Frank sighed. "Now, I'm back to square one."

"As soon as they get the fire out we'll search the remains of the body for any written clues," the agent said. "I'll get the sheriff to rope off the accident scene. When it's daylight we'll go over the area carefully."

The following morning, Frank rose shortly before dawn. Waking several times during the night, he decided to give up further attempts at sleep and went downstairs for coffee. At the first rays of the sun, Frank left the house and drove to the accident scene. Being the first to arrive, he slowly walked the area, looking for anything that might provide information to where this guy came from. The badly burned body had been removed the previous night and Frank held little hope that anything readable would be found. He had been about ready to depart when he decided to walk a wider area away from the wreck hoping that something might have been flung out during the impact. As he circled the area, kicking the leaves with his feet, he felt something hard. Just as he started to reach down two FBI vehicles drove up.

Agent Philips got out of the first car. "Couldn't wait," he teased. "Find anything?"

"Nothing yet," Frank lied. He wanted to examine the solid object beneath his foot before he showed it to the agents in case they would later try to keep its significance from him until they thought he should know. Besides, he told himself, it may be nothing more than a rock or a piece of trash.

While the agents, wearing white gloves, shifted through the remains of the wrecked car thirty feet away, Frank turned his back to them and reached down and picked up a relatively new cell phone. Except for a few nicks and scratches, it looked undamaged. It had to be from the wrecked car, he told himself. Holding his breath, he pushed the redial button on the phone. After a split second, he heard the distinct sound of automatic dialing.

"General Fenton's office. Can I help you?"

Frank nearly dropped the phone. His heart raced. Then that *was* him I heard over the pay phone, Frank thought. But he's been dead for decades.

"Hello, hello," the secretary said.

Frank slowly replaced the receiver to his ear. "Fenton? Is that . . . Miles Fenton?"

"That's correct. General Miles Fenton."

"Is he an aviator?"

"This is an unlisted number. How did you obtain it?" The secretary replied, ignoring the previous question.

Frank clicked off the cell phone as Agent Philips walked up to him.

"Calling your wife for coffee?" Philips said. "I sure could use some."

"No, I was just phoning a ghost. The redial button on this cell phone led me to the man who's been hiring these guys," Frank said as he handed the phone to Philip. "I found it lying on the ground."

"Oh, no," Philips grabbed the phone from Frank and put it into a transparent plastic bag. "Don't you know not to mess with evidence?" Philips scolded. "Your prints may have overlapped those of the dead guy. Without those prints, we can't legally prove that there's a connection between the hired killer and whoever you talked to on that phone."

"Oh, shit," Frank replied softly. "I'm sorry." He knew he had goofed. But at least he now knew who his adversary was. And Frank knew he was probably the only person alive on earth who knew why his tormentor wanted him dead.

9

The third meeting with Coffey took place in Frank's house. Agent Philips also was present along with Nicole.

"Your stories are getting weirder by the day," Coffey said. "You're telling me that a four-star general has been paying these hit men to have you killed."

"You got the cell phone. Just hit the redial button," Frank replied.

"We already did."

"And?"

"It was General Fenton's unlisted number."

"I rest my case," Frank said firmly.

"Okay, we know that." Coffey glared at Frank. "But because of your handling the phone with your bare hands, we don't have any prints on the phone other than yours. We can't connect it to the hit man as a result."

Nicole sat up and interrupted. "Wouldn't it seem strange to a jury that General what-ever-his name, has his unlisted number on a nearly new cell phone lying in a field near the car wreck of an assassin?"

"Not if the defense claimed that Frank planted the phone to frame the general," Coffey countered.

"Oh." Nicole shrugged and leaned back again in the sofa.

Coffey started to pace the room, his fingers rubbing his chin, "Let's put this in perspective. You're accusing a four-star general of leading a murderous band of drug smugglers in Vietnam and hiring assassins thirty years later to kill you."

"Yes, sir. Only back then he was a captain," Frank said.

"Why hasn't anybody else come forward with this information since then?"

"Everyone connected to it is dead, or at least I thought, until Fenton turned up alive."

"So he's trying to kill you to keep you from blowing the whistle on his past, I suppose?"

"That has to be his reason," Frank said.

"Then why did he wait thirty years?"

"I didn't know he was alive."

"Exactly. Until he tried to have you assassinated. Right?"

Frank nodded.

Coffey stood up and raised a finger in the air. "Doesn't make sense, does it? He, in effect, blew his cover. Why, after all this time?"

"I don't know," Frank answered, shaking his head.

A third FBI agent knocked on the front door and entered. He whispered into the ear of Coffey and showed him a printout. Coffey scratched his head and turned toward Frank and Nicole. Whatever pugnacity he had left, vanished.

"We ran a check on General Fenton. He's a hot potato."

"Meaning?" Frank asked.

"Tomorrow, the President is going to nominate General Miles Fenton as the new Chairman of the Joint Chiefs of Staff."

Frank stood and pointed at Coffey. "There's our reason. He had to act to silence me because his name will be on the news and I would've found out that he's still alive."

Coffey defensively looked at both Frank and Nicole. "For the first time, that makes sense."

Nicole sat back in her chair, folded her arms, and eyed Coffey with a 'I told you so,' stare.'

Frank sat down and then immediately jumped up. "We've got to stop the appointment."

Coffey shook his head timidly back and forth. "Only the Senate hearings on the nomination can do that."

"When do they begin?"

"Next week."

"What can we do?" Frank asked.

"We have no proof that the voice on the telephone belonged to General Fenton, only your word," Coffey said. "And it's your story about him in Vietnam. But without witnesses and the assassin prints on that phone, your accusation is weak. Best I can do now is get you a list of committee members and let you fax them your challenge to his nomination."

"Isn't there any way we can connect Fenton with this?" Frank said.

"How?" Coffey answered. "We can't even prove who these dead guys are. Right now all we have is a case of self-defense against a guy that could've been just a park robber and another man who sped away from home after hitting you. The only reason we're allowed to be involved now is because of your statement that the first guy claimed to be an FBI agent."

10

Frank sat alone on a lawn chair in the rear of his house in the early evening. A slight breeze carried the cool fall air over the long manicured lawn from the lake but he paid scant attention to its pleasant caress. A multitude of thoughts whirled through his mind. How did Fenton survive a sure death? What can I prove against him without witnesses or corroborating evidence? It would be my word against him and I'm practically an outcast airline pilot still under suspicion of attempted suicide.

An approaching sound interrupted his thoughts. He looked up and watched a helicopter skimming low over the river. As it started to pass his property, it took a ninety-degree turn toward him, came to a hover, and gently sat down on the grass about forty yards from him. The helicopter, a Bell 0H-58, was painted olive drab and had black letters on its side spelling out 'United States Army.'

What in the hell, Frank thought. An emergency landing? He heard the engine spool down but it didn't stop completely. Frank watched as a uniformed figure got out of the craft while the blades were still slowly rotating. Frank, puzzled, stood up as the person approached him. Thirty years had passed but Frank immediately recognized the man.

"You," Frank said.

General Miles Fenton, 57, tall and distinguished looking in an officer's uniform, resplendent with clusters of awards, badges and four stars on his shoulder boards, held out his hand. Frank ignored it.

"How in hell did you survive?" Frank said.

"To put it in a nutshell," the general replied calmly, "the explosion blew me out through the latrine window into the brush, buck ass naked. When they found me later, the Army immediately shipped me to a burns hospital in Japan before they even knew who I was. That's where I regained consciousness. By that time you had rotated back to the stateside hospital and out of the Army. Nobody knew of my past activities and I continued my career, quite lucratively, I may add."

"That's going to end quite soon." Frank said emphatically.

"You don't understand. I'm here to call a truce. To make a deal." The general waved his arm around Frank's property. "You haven't done badly yourself."

"You expect me to deal with my brother's murderer?" Frank said, his anger intensifying.

"I had nothing to do with your brother's death."

"Bull."

The general shrugged and appeared apologetic. "Trust me on this. Sergeant Wilson shot your brother. I didn't even know about it until after it was over. But look, let's not fight over things in the past. I heard you need money to pay off your debts and to keep this place and I'm the guy who can supply it."

"I'm taking you down, " Frank moved closer to Fenton. "You tried to kill over a hundred passengers just to get me."

"You're not listening, mister," the general said, referring to Frank's old rank. "I got something else to offer you, something precious."

"Forget it."

"I'm offering you Nicole's life."

Frank was stunned. Then he angrily stepped closer to Fenton who backed away and placed his hand in a jacket pocket. "Careful, I'm armed." He smiled when Frank stopped.

"You even try to lay a hand on her and I'll —."

"The next man I send will be more professional," Fenton interrupted. "She's dead meat unless you cooperate."

The remark captured Frank's complete attention. "Leave her alone. It's me you want."

"The general's shrugged. "Sure, I can do that. And to sweeten the pot, I can give you, say, a million in cash, untaxed, payable when you don't show up for the hearing and forget that you ever knew me."

"Just where will you get that kind of money?"

Fenton, now more relaxed, eagerly sat down on the lawn chair next to Frank. "Guess how much defense industries will pay for insider data on a multi-billion dollar defense contract. And that's just the tip of the iceberg on ways to get money when you're a four-star." He stood up and again offered Frank his hand. "A deal?"

Frank stood up and answered with a right cross to Fenton's mouth and the general went down. Fenton, slightly dazed, picked himself up slowly and wiped the blood from his lips with the back of his hand. "That's for my brother, you liar," Frank said.

As Fenton regained his senses, his eyes glared at Frank with rage. Blood dribbled down his chin. "You just signed your wife's death certificate. But first, I'll ruin you in the hearings. Everyone will think you're a nut case. You'll never fly with any airline again." Fenton fingered what was obviously a gun in his pocket. "If I wasn't here with that pilot," he said, looking toward the waiting copter, "I'd take care of you now. But mark my words, you and your family are going live in fear of your lives."

"Oh yeah. You're forgetting about two CIA agents. Chuck and Al and the term 'Dragnet.' Those senators are going to get an earful."

The general trotted back toward the still-running helicopter. He stopped and shouted. "You fool. Can't you figure it out? Nobody's alive except you. Those two agents died in a helicopter crash on the day you rotated. They didn't get a chance to finish their report on me. Our mission was such a hot, illegal potato with Congress, the CIA quietly destroyed all its 'Dragnet' files thirty years ago. There's nothing left but my word against a mentally unbalanced, out-of-work pilot."

The general entered the helicopter and it lifted off into the dark sky.

11

Frank stood at the kitchen sink holding his bruised hand under the faucet. Nicole, returning home from the hospital, entered through the front door. When she heard the running water, she sauntered into the kitchen. That's when she saw Frank's scraped and bloody knuckles. "My God, your hand?"

"You should have seen the ghost I punched."

Nicole gave a nervous laugh. "Okay, I'll bite, what's going on?"

Frank turned and held Nicole by the shoulders. "General Fenton was here."

Nicole gave Frank a skeptical look. She didn't like to hear things like that, not at this time, especially when she had regained her faith in her husband. Maybe it was Frank's idea of a joke, she thought. A poor one, but a joke nevertheless.

Frank shook his head. "I wished you had arrived home just a little bit earlier to be a witness that he was here. He flew here by copter and claimed that there would be no record of his use of that bird on this day."

"You're not kidding, then." Nicole studied Frank's face. "Okay, assuming that he came to see you, what did he want?"

"He offered me your life plus a million not to testify. You see my answer on these knuckles."

Nicole lowered her voice as though the world was listening. "He threatened to kill me?"

Frank turned away from Nicole and continued running water over his hand. "Unless I kill him first."

Nicole reached out and spun Frank around to face her. "You'll go to prison if you do that."

"Either way, I lose," Frank said.

Nicole nervously paced back and forth across the room. "I don't understand. How can this be happening to us?" She looked at Frank with scolding eyes as if he had admitted to having an affair with another woman. "How did you ever get involved with this man?"

"It's a long story."

Nicole stopped her pacing and stared angrily at Frank. "You better tell me what happened over there."

"Maybe it's time you knew."

"I'd say so since my life is now on the line."

Frank motioned for Nicole to follow him into the family room. There, he plopped heavily into a chair and looked pensively at his wife. God, he couldn't stand the thought of anything happening to her. How could she have ever known about the garbage attached to the guy she married. He had never told her about his brief tour in Vietnam. He had always considered it ancient history and best forgotten.

"I don't know where to begin," Frank said.

"How about the beginning," Nicole anxiously urged. She loved her career as a surgeon, helping people to live longer and better. But outside of Frank, she never had acquaintances of the adventurous type. Now she was involved in a big and dangerous game, and to her surprise, she loved it.

"I never told you much about my brother, have I?" Frank began.

"Only that he was killed in Vietnam."

Frank looked away from Nicole and stared across the room as though he could see the image of the figure he was talking about. "He was more than an older brother. He was my friend, my mentor, a replacement for my father who, as you know, died when I was five." Frank paused for a second, swallowed as if he was trying to hold back his emotions, before continuing. "He did everything for me. Did I ever tell you that he was the one that dove into that swift flowing river to rescue me? Every kid had a hero and he was mine. I loved him."

Nicole, feeling his emotions, sat silently.

Frank sifted uneasily in his chair and looked down at the floor. "And when he needed me the most, I turned my back on him."

"Why?" Nicole asked quietly.

Frank continued to look at the floor. "He volunteered for 'Nam. Said it was time for his turn in the barrel— that everybody had to help their country during a war."

"What's so wrong with that?"

"It was a war I and my friends were actively protesting against in college. You see, at that age we felt privileged, smart, and thought we knew an unjust war when we saw it. I warned him not to volunteer because he would be aiding the war effort and that he would cause our mother unnecessary worry. That he was being duped by the establishment and that he must be pretty dumb not to recognize that fact."

Frank looked up at Nicole with moist eyes. "On his last day at home . . . he asked me to drive him to the airport. I refused. Pushed him away when he tried to give me a hug. I called him a baby killer and walked away."

Frank hung his head down. "That was the last time I ever saw him alive." Frank, still looking down, put his head in his hands. "I was so self-righteous then."

Nicole came to his side and placed an arm around his shoulders. "A lot of people acted that way about the war. You weren't alone in your feelings."

Frank paused a second to regain his composure. "When we received word he was missing in action, I was grief-stricken. Talk about regret. That last day with him had already begun to haunt me . . . . God, if I could only relive that moment."

"Must have been horrible for you," Nicole said consolingly.

"I thought if I could try . . . to find him, I could live with myself."

"That's why you volunteered?"

Frank nodded. "A fool's errand. Once I got over there, I saw how impossible it would be to find a missing soldier. Then I met those two guys."

"Who were they?" Nicole asked.

"I'm getting to that." Frank got up from the sofa and went to the kitchen returning minutes later with two cups of coffee. He gave one to Nicole and sat down. "This is not a short story," he explained. "I met those two when I received orders at my unit in Nha Trang to go to Saigon to meet with Group S2. That's security."

12

"When I arrived in Saigon that night, a mixture of military and commercial aircraft were parked in front of a long, one-story terminal building. I had only been in-country two days before I got the orders and everything was strange and new to me."

"I remember how surprised I was when I entered the terminal and found it nearly empty. I wore civilian clothes and worried that the Army personnel who were supposed to pick me up might overlook my presence." Frank looked at Nicole and smiled ruefully. "Are you sure you want to hear all of this?"

"You're not sleeping in our bedroom, unless—."

Frank nodded, indicating he got the picture.

"Well, I settled in a chair for what I thought would be a long night when two men came and stood behind me."

"Ready to go?" A man's voice said.

I turned around and saw two civilian construction types in blue jump suits and white plastic safety helmets.

"You got the wrong man, I'm military."

"That's obvious," the stouter of the two men replied. "You haircut's a dead giveaway." He acted more like he was making an arrest rather than an inquiry.

I looked carefully at the two men. One was stout and the other skinny.

"You're also Frank Braden," the man continued. "I'm Chuck and this is my associate, Al. "We have a car outside."

"Group sent you?" I asked.

"You could say that."

The men in their late thirties slid into position on both sides of me and escorted me to the exit. Al, the nervous skinny guy got behind the wheel and the beefy Chuck sat in the front passenger seat. I got in the rear seat.

Our auto sped deep into the interior of the city. I thought Al drove with more luck than skill. The roadway ran through an urban area where darkness was interrupted only by widely scattered streetlights. Lights from the open doors of the bars and small shops silhouetted figures and objects on the sidewalk. An endless procession of motor scooters and motorbikes, carrying one or two young men, sputtered past at breakneck speeds, their small headlights revealing the smoky vapors from the tailpipes in front of them. Fumes and the unrelenting beeping of vehicle horns surrounded their auto.

"How far is it to Group?"

Chuck turned around. "We're not going to Group."

I leaned forward, confused. "Why not?"

"This will be your briefing. It's for your own safety," Chuck answered in a warning voice. "Everything we say must not get beyond this car."

I exchanged glances with both Chuck and the guy called Al. "Wait a minute, what's going on? Didn't Group send you?"

"We're from the Company, CIA to you."

"You sure you got the right man?"

"For our sake, we sure hope so," Chuck answered while Al nodded.

Silence followed the exchange. I leaned back into seat, completely puzzled. I looked out the window, trying to see some recognizable building or landmark in case I had to quickly exit the car. On each side of the road, adjoining two and three-story white masonry buildings boxed in the street. Some had apartment balconies displaying decorative railings like those in New Orleans. On the ground floors were small jewelry and clothing stores, repair shops, nondescript bars and mom and pop size restaurants with room for only three or four tables.

Cheap looking hotels with no lobbies were sandwiched in between the shops. Alleyways were jammed with open food markets and the smell of fermented fish filtered through the car. On the sidewalk, middle-aged women wearing conical hats stirred boiling sauce in pots over open fires. They cooked barefooted and all had dirty white blouses hanging over black pantaloon pants as though it were some kind of uniform. Some were handing steaming wooded bowls of rice, fish and vegetables to customers squatting near the curb. Trees grew from symmetrical holes in the sidewalk to give a French décor to the scene.

I didn't know where in the hell I was.

"It ain't Paris," Chuck said after observing me staring out the window.

I turned to Chuck. "Say, you guys never showed me any identification."

"Didn't think we had to," Chuck said, "Who do you think we are—native VC?" He and Al roared with laughter.

The laugh from Al froze in his throat. He swore as he blew the horn, simultaneously braking and turning the wheel to miss a yellow Peugeot taxi that had cut in front of their vehicle. Al skidded the vehicle into a curb with a thump, scattering the sidewalk entrepreneurs. Women dropped their wooden spoons and ran back from the street along with their formerly squatting clients. A half block from where the car came to a halt, a fortune-teller clutching a small cage with a black crow inside, jumped up and waved a deck of cards at the intruding vehicle, while cursing in his native tongue.

Sweet Jesus, I thought, if we had skidded onto the sidewalk, we'd be here five years from now explaining to surviving relatives, MPs and those white glove Vietnamese police what had happened.

As Al pulled the auto away from the curb, Chuck broke the silence. "We want your help."

"I don't understand?"

Didn't you work as a reporter for a Cincinnati newspaper and fly for the Army National Guard before you volunteered to come on active duty?"

"Sure, but journalism was only a temporary career for me. I plan to fly fulltime, hopefully with an airline."

"Nevertheless," Chuck pointed out, "You got investigative reporting experience; you're a military pilot, and—thanks to us—you've been assigned to the 119th. You got a legitimate assignment. You're above suspicion."

"Where is this leading?"

"It's simple. We need the names of some bad guys in the 119th."

I shifted uncomfortably in my seat. "Can't your organization do that?"

Chuck shook his head. "A section of your unit is performing a valuable covert mission in a country we're not supposed to be in."

Al turned around and nodded in agreement. "Listen soldier, the doves in Congress would raise hell about it if they knew. An official investigation is out of the question."

Chuck took a deep breath and shrugged. "We suspect your unit is flying more drug sorties than legitimate missions—."

"That's right, soldier" Al said, interrupting his partner, "we call your outfit, 'Air Opium.'"

"We're pretty sure they're using our Army planes to fly poppy crops from isolated Laotian villages to a Corsican processing lab in Vientiane," Chuck explained.

I turned away and looked out the window. Why did they pick on me? I don't have time for this. I turned around. "I got my own problems. Just pull over to the curb. I'll catch a cab."

The car slowed but didn't stop. Al leaned over and whispered into Chuck's ear. They both nodded and Chuck turned around again. "Doesn't the thought of doing a vital job for your country, inspire you?"

Boy, did these guys select the wrong person. I decided to take the diplomatic way out. "Don't get me wrong. It's not that I'm not unaware of the importance of the problem you have, but I got enough to occupy me right now." I paused, wondering if I should tell them the truth why I really volunteered for Vietnam. I figured it couldn't hurt. May even help if they could give me some tips on finding missing persons. And boy, did they.

"You see, in my family my brother was the gung-ho type, not me. And he disappeared over here while working for the CID. I only volunteered for active duty to come over here to look for him."

Both agents looked at each other but remained silent.

"I understand," Chuck said finally, breaking the silence.

It was then that I began having an uncomfortable feeling that there was more than what these two had told me. To kill time, I again looked at the passing mènage as my eyes adjusted to the darkness. Young, attractive, dainty boned women in colorful ao dai gowns, split at the waist and worn over silky long-legged pants, strolled the sidewalk past skinny uni-formed Vietnamese men who stood around watching them. Also taking up sidewalk space were larger American GIs and the bands of giggling, barefoot street urchins who followed them, like homeless jack-als, trying to sneak up during an unguarded moment to swipe the elastic band watches from their wrists. It was all quite fascinating.

Chuck again broke the silence. "We need your help, bad."

This time I came up with a better answer. I hadn't expected to get off the hook that easy and had wondered when they would try their sales spiel again. "Hey, come on, I'm just a Peter pilot now and that's the way I want to keep it. What about your own people? I'm not a trained spook."

Chuck was pleading now. "We don't have anybody with your background. We tried to infiltrate another man and he's disappeared."

"The answer is no."

"Wait a minute. I'm not through. I want to tell you about the last guy we sent," Chuck said, his eyes narrow-ing. "He gave up his life for the chance to end this. He's missing but we know he's dead. He's an unsung hero."

Al nodded in agreement.

"That's exactly how I don't want to end up," I shot back. "Look, I'm sorry about him. But at least he was trained for it and had a chance. You want me to risk my neck to root out some smugglers who'll kill to protect themselves."

"Why not? If my brother got murdered, I'd do it," Chuck said.

That statement melted my defense quicker than an ice cube dropped in boiling water. My mouth went dry and I leaned slowly back into the seat while I tried to comprehend what was just told me.

"You can't mean my brother. Jack wasn't in the CIA," I said weakly.

"The Army CID loaned him to us. He volunteered. We sent him to the 119th under the name of Pat Burnside, a clerk specialist. As soon as they discovered who he really was, they killed him."

I stared hard at Chuck. Almost a full minute of silence followed. Al remained quiet and kept his eyes on the road ahead.

"You knew I came to find him."

Chuck nodded.

"You think he's dead?"

Chuck nodded.

I shouted at them in bitter anger, tears streaming down my face. "Why weren't we told? Can't you imagine what my mother has been going through."

"We couldn't disclose his mission and we don't have his body, yet." Chuck said softly.

"Then he still could be alive?"

Chuck shook his head slowly. "Now will you help us to get his killers?"

"Where's his body?"

"If you can find an excuse for your company to probe

92

the bottom of an oil pit where he was last seen, I think you'll find him."

I swallowed hard. My quest for my brother's forgiveness was over. And I failed. Now I was stuck in Viet Nam for a year. Then a slow burning anger came over me. Now that I was here it would give me a chance to avenge my brother. After a few minutes, I replied, "What do you want me to do?"

A look of relief came over Chuck. "For your safety, nobody in the military will be aware of your connection to us. Don't get too inquisitive. Be cool and patient. Don't keep notes; we think that's how they discovered your brother's identity. Get us the names of who's involved and how they operate and we'll do the rest."

"Who do I contact?"

"We'll contact you."

Al stopped the car a short distance from the Brink's Officers Quarters and I stepped out. The car pulled away and I watched the taillights fade into the darkness, feeling very alone and full of sorrow.

Frank turned and looked at Nicole who sat mesmerized on the sofa. "The next day I had my first encounter with Captain Fenton, our XO. I went to see the company commander, Major Clements, but he wasn't in his office. At that time I didn't know if Fenton was part of the smugglers so I took no chances. I gave him a phony story why Group S2 wanted to see me. Boy, I still can visualize the look on Fenton's face."

13

The 119th Aviation Company headquarters was a metal Quonset hut that sat among a forest of Quonset huts at the Nha Trang Airbase. It was noon as I walked through the deserted company orderly room to Major Clements' office. The office was empty and so I turned around to leave.

Fenton, then 27, dressed in spotless fatigues and shining boots, came out of his office. "Looking for something, Mister Braden?"

"Major Clements. Guess he's not back from lunch, huh?"

"We haven't been introduced but I'm Captain Miles Fenton, the Executive Officer." I'll never forget his look. He stared at me with a facial expression of a maitre d' greeting a less affluent diner. I offered my hand but he did not extend his. And believe me, there's nothing that irritates me more than having my arm and hand extended out into empty space and being deliberately ignored. That showed me he was a jerk so I retaliated quickly. I sniffed the air, knowing that he had lots of aftershave lotion on. "This place smells like perfume."

"That's my aftershave lotion, Mister."

That said, I simply shrugged my shoulders and walked toward the door. "Sorry 'bout that. I'll come back when the major's here."

Fenton's faced turned a shade of pink. He motioned with his hand for me to return. "I'm the commander when the major is out. So, tell me. What did the Group Intelligence want with you?"

"Just a security check."

"Explain that."

"It's rather a private matter," I said nonchalantly. This was really one person I could sense that I would never respect, so I made it as hard as possible for him to get a direct answer.

Fenton's face went from pink to red. "Nothing's private in the Army, Mister. You either tell me or I'll stand you at attention until you do."

I looked down, coughed, picked up a desk ashtray, examined it and replaced it while my mind raced to invent a story. "Okay, but it's not a pretty story," I lied. "You see, I flew for the National Guard and worked as a reporter. I mixed up the names of a robber and the man he robbed. The paper got sued and I got canned. So, I volunteered for a year of active duty to keep employed. G2 wanted the details about my dismissal. I guess to make sure it didn't involve drugs or alcohol." I shrugged my shoulders and displayed a sheepish grin. I really didn't think it wasn't too bad of a phony story to think up in that short time. And he fell for it.

A smirk along with a look of relief crossed Fenton's face. "I expect to be addressed with a 'sir' in the future, mister. And for your information, the Army isn't a refuge for rejects. Screw up here and I'll have you court-martialed."

"Yes sir," I said smartly. I snapped to attention, saluted, and did a military about face, and marched toward the door with a grin on my face. If he wants formal military, I'll give it to him in basketfuls.

Fenton leaned forward with both hands on the desk he stood behind, not quite sure if he had succeeded in reminding this Warrant Officer pilot of military etiquette or whether he was being mocked. "Wait a minute. How did you get this assignment, anyway? This is considered a choice job over here. Usually given to second tour pilots," he said with a suspicious reflection in his voice.

I paused at the doorway, still grinning, "Lucky, I guess—sir."

"I'm having you assigned up north to the Marble Mountain platoon near Da Nang. If you came in the Army looking for excitement, you'll find it up there."

I didn't expect that and quickly replied. "I'd rather stay here at headquarters." *Where I can keep an eye on things and locate my brother's body.*

"Too bad. Dismissed."

Frank looked at an engrossed Nicole. "Of course, not having the expertise of a James Bond, I probably blew my cover within the next few days, especially when I told our company commander, Major Clements, in secret where I thought my brother's body was hidden."

Nicole quickly asked if Major Clements was part of the smugglers, too.

"Naw. He was a great guy, really. A barrel chest six-footer, who was the worst accordion player you ever heard. He was a guy you wouldn't want to cross but he would go to bat for you if you were right. He was an honest man, but unfortunately he had a crook as an executive officer who handled most of the company's paperwork along with the First Sergeant. And he had to work with his executive officer to recover the body.

But my sudden appearance in the company probably aroused their suspicions, anyways."

"Didn't you suspect Fenton right off?"

"There was no indication of his involvement at first. That came later. I can only surmise what they said about me when they met secretly in those first few days."

14

"My cover was really blown, though, when they found my brother's body exactly where I told them it would be. Major Clements apparently thought that my request for him to keep it a secret as to who told him where to locate my brother's body didn't include keeping it from his staff."

"When the smugglers found out that you knew where the body was they would've killed you if you had been around," Nicole said with a worried frown.

Frank shook his head. "They would need to make it look like an accident or make me disappear forever like they thought they had done to my brother. So, they needed time to formulate a plan."

"Any more creepy characters?" Nicole asked.

"The most fascinating one was Lan, a brothel owner and co-conspirator who arranged the purchase deals between the Laotian poppy growers and the Corsicans who operated the labs in Vientiane. Unknown to all, he was also a colonel in the Viet Cong. I met him on my first trip to Laos."

Frank looked sadly at Nicole. "When they found my brother's body, we were landing in Vientiane. Later, I heard that the CID arrived at the oil pond and quickly took it away for shipment to the States."

"What was Laos like?" Nicole asked.

"Like Vientiane," Frank answered.

"Okay, smarty, what was Vientiane like?"

"A hodgepodge of drugs, soldiers of fortune, enemy and allied diplomats, bars and brothels, and spies, all drawn together by a clandestine war with all sides living together in the city."

"Tell me about this Lan character."

"I figured he was the key to this whole smuggling operation so I sought him out the first chance I had by going to his place of business."

15

When I entered the door of Lannie's early that afternoon in Vientiane I didn't know what to expect there at that time of day. But it was better than sitting around the hotel waiting for Tom Parker, my roommate, to return from a flight which I suspected involved picking up another load of poppies. These flight were only flown by those in their syndicate. Besides, I figured Lan might hold some interesting information that I planned to get out of him. He might even think I recently joined the smugglers since I was traveling with Tom.

An overhead light behind the bar provided the only illumination inside. I paused momentarily in the doorway to adjust my eyes to the dimness. I could almost taste the stale cigarette smoke lingering from the previous night. A falsetto voice was singing Vietnamese lyrics in an unfamiliar rhythmic beat. I looked around and found the sound coming from a small, black, three-band portable radio sitting on the bar.

Across the empty dance floor, I saw Lan, slouched in a chair at a table. I figured him to be about forty-five. He wore a knitted dark polyester suit and a pink shirt with a brown striped tie. His thick black hair sat in a sprayed pompadour and an expensive watch wrapped itself around his thick wrist. A diamond protruded out from a ring on his little finger. He looked more like a pimp than a VC colonel commanding three crack battalions near Saigon

He seemed to be in deep meditation, staring at the empty stage. A half full teacup sat at his elbow. I stopped slightly behind the silent form and cleared my throat to announce my presence. "Good afternoon. Let me introduce my—."

"I know who you are, Mister Braden," the figure said without turning around. "You are the new pilot."

Lan turned around and looked at me with eyes that expressed sadness. He had deep, penetrating dark eyes that showed an overwhelming presence of command and composure. In his right hand was a Chicom automatic pistol. "Please sit down."

I saw the pistol and remained standing. "I'm looking for Tom Parker." I motioned toward the pistol. "Could you put that away?"

Lan smiled and placed the pistol in a pocket. I then sat down.

"Sorry. I was trying to determine whether I needed to defend myself," Lan said apologetically.

"Hey, I'm Parker's friend, remember?"

"You also, I believe, are connected to the CIA. Is that not true?" Lan said decisively.

I rubbed the back of my neck, grimaced and shrugged, trying to figure out how to answer that. So I answered his question with a question. "What makes you say that?"

"I have informants in Saigon."

At my first close up glance of Lan's face, I told myself that I would learn little that Lan did not want me to know. "I'm not an agent per se."

"I can see that now. One cannot be too careful. You might have been on an assassination assignment."

"I'm glad we cleared that up."

"So what on earth brought you to Southeast Asia?" Lan inquired.

"Uncle Sam." I wondered if Lan would know who Uncle Sam was.

"Oh yes, your omnipotent Uncle. Savior of the cultures of the world," he said bitterly. Lan paused and sipped his coffee. "Tell me, why do Americans like you want to aid a small, insignificant puppet nation ruled by criminals?"

"Who says I want to aid North Vietnam?" *I might not be jumping for joy over my presence here, but I am not that wet behind the ears to think that North Vietnam did nothing to promote the conflict.*

Lan shifted uneasily in his seat and studied me. "I do not like your humor, Mister Braden. Do you not realize you are defending corrupt Saigon puppets?"

"We didn't choose the battleground. They did. I think we simply selected the lesser of two evils."

Lan ignored the statement by changing the subject. "Are you here to rent one of my girls?"

The question caught me off guard and I laughed. "No. I kinda like to mix love in with my sex."

"Oh yes, love," Lan injected with bland indifference. One of the few things our cultures do not collide on."

"In your business I didn't think the word meant much."

"It may surprise you, Mister Braden," Lan paused and looked away toward the dark stage again. "Years ago, I was a French trained school teacher out in the provinces, in love with what I thought was the most interesting, beautiful woman in my world." He turned and looked at me. "I was about your age then, full of expectations. We had a baby who was my daughter."

"Where are they now?"

"French warplanes, out on a reprisal raid . . . hit our village thinking we had become too friendly with the Vietminh. Many were killed. She and my daughter among them—I never looked back again at that side of life."

"I'm sorry."

"I joined the Vietminh shortly afterwards and helped drive the French out of my country. Later, I was bored with the rhetoric and regimentation of the self-serving leaders in the North and headed south into this business."

Lan seemed so forthright and easy with his answers, I decided this was the time to toss out a hook. "If you don't mind my asking, does that include drugs, too?"

Lan's eyes didn't waver and he showed no facial emotions to the question. "Mister Braden, everybody handles drugs in the golden triangle. Life here—from the poor Melo farmer who harvests the poppies to the customer who uses it in my bar—it's legal here and a way of life."

"You don't care for the Saigon government today, do you?"

"They are not much different than when the French told them what to do."

"If you don't care for them why are you working with the American pilots here?"

"It is profitable," Lan said.

"Then they're in the drug business with you?"

Lan rose out of his chair. "I am sorry we cannot talk more. Mister Parker left a message that you are to meet at the plane this afternoon at three."

"Too late I realized that it was me, not Lan, who provided answers to unasked questions."

Nicole eyes were riveted on Frank. "I can see why it didn't take you too long to get shot. Who shot you?"

"Another drug smuggler I hadn't suspected."

"What happened to Fenton?"

"Near the end of his tour, Fenton got hoggish and planned to assassinate Lan to avoid the payments they owed him. Actually, someone else tried to assassinate Lan but he thought Fenton was responsible. So he turned the tables on them."

"How do you mean?"

"He used his VC to track 'em all down and kill them. I thought when I was medevaced back to the States because of my wound, that all my brother's killers were dead. But, somehow, Fenton escaped."

"All this intrigue in the middle of a war," Nicole questioned. "Where were the enemy soldiers all this time?"

Frank gave her a wry smile. "Believe me, they were all around, inside and outside of our bases. In fact, Lan had all his bets covered since he suspected there might be a double-cross when his American co-smugglers neared their DEROS date. He had explosives planted under a half-million gallon fuel storage tank right adjacent to Fenton's barracks for such an event."

"How did he manage to do that?"

"He used his Viet Cong troops to tunnel under the aviation fuel storage tank and plant a 500-pound unexploded American bomb they found in the jungle.

"Later I found out that our intelligence message section had intercepted a coded communication sent from Nha Trang to the North Vietnamese Embassy in Laos to a Colonel Binh Lan that the dragon would exhale fire at his command. Of course the decoders had no idea where the explosives were planted."

After listening to Frank's stories in astonishment, Nicole turned serious. "Now, what are we going to do about Fenton. He seems almost indestructible."

"For the moment, yes. But there's bound to be a chink in his armor. We just have to find it."

Nicole face was full of doubt. "How?"

Their thoughts were interrupted by noise from the fax machine in the study. Frank jumped up quickly from the sofa and went into the room. Nicole came up behind him as he read a sheet of paper.

"What's in the fax?"

Frank looking glum, handed her the fax. "It's from our favorite FBI nemesis, Coffey. He confirms Al and Chuck were killed in a plane crash shortly after I left 'Nam. Worse, he says the CIA claims they never heard of 'Dragnet' and have nothing in their files on it."

"Then the general wasn't lying." Nicole said as she looked over the fax.

Frank nodded. "Look at the last paragraph. Coffey says he has no substantial evidence linking anything to Fenton. He also cites that Fenton's private office number in the cell phone I found is not proof because I contaminated the evidence and could've planted the number myself."

"This all means what?" Nicole asked.

"That he can't help me at the hearing. I have to face Fenton and those Senators alone." Frank turned and stared at a framed photograph showing a WestSky Airliner flying over the nation's Capitol Building.

16

Frank and Nicole walked up the steps to the Senate Building and entered a large atrium. After making inquires at the information desk, they proceeded down a long hallway to the hearing room. At the door they showed identification to a Senate Sergeant of Arms guarding the entrance.

Frank was directed to a small table in front of a long, elevated table of seven Senators and their aides. Nicole took a seat in a row of chairs behind him. To her left and several rows behind her were General Fenton and his attorney. The Senate majority leader, Senator Pike, a tall slender man about sixty, occupied the middle seat in front of a microphone.

Senator Pike cleared his throat and moved the mike closer to him. "Mister Braden, I received a fax from you concerning the appointment of General Miles Fenton to the post of Chairman of the Joint Chiefs of Staff."

The Senator took off his glasses and looked down at Frank. "These are serious charges. That is why we called this closed hearing prior to the confirmation hearing. Can you prove any of these?"

"That's why I'm here, sir," Frank said firmly.

Senator Pike glanced at his colleagues, put on his

glasses and looked at the papers on his desk. "You claim that General Fenton paid an assassin to plant a bomb aboard your airliner to prevent you from testifying against his appointment. Is that correct, sir?"

"Yes, sir."

"How many people were aboard your aircraft at the time?"

"One hundred and ten, sir."

Senator Pike again removed his glasses and looked quizzically at Frank. "Wouldn't you agree that's a bit of an overkill just to eliminate you?"

"I think they were trying to make my death look like a suicide, sir."

"And what brought you to this conclusion?"

"John Doe, sir."

"And who is this John Doe?" Pike said patiently.

"He's a yet-to-be identified man I shot in self-defense. We think he planted the bomb on my plane. I found a coded phone number on his body to a public pay phone here in Washington. The code gave a specific time and date to call the number."

"Did you call the number?"

"Yes, sir. General Fenton, I believe, answered the phone."

There was a murmur among the Senators and their aides that was interrupted by a shout from the back of the room by Fenton's attorney. "I object to this slander. This man has no proof, no backing from FBI investigators that General Fenton had any connection to that phone number."

Pike rapped the gavel on his desk. "Please sit down, counsel. This is not a trial. You can refute these accusations when your turn comes."

"Did General Fenton identify himself?"

"No, sir," Frank answered, "but I recognized the voice."

"Prior to the phone call, how long had it been since you last heard General Fenton's voice?"

"About thirty years."

"Thirty years!" the Senator blurted.

"It's easy to remember the voice of a man who murdered my brother in Vietnam."

Senator Pike adjusted his glasses again. "Are you accusing General Fenton of murdering your brother?"

"Yes, sir. General Fenton, then Captain Fenton, was responsible for my brother's death in 1967. Captain Fenton, unknown to his superiors, was the leader of a military clique of opium smugglers in Vietnam. My brother, CWO Jack Braden, was on undercover assignment with the CIA to break up the ring. When Fenton discovered his true identify, he had him killed."

"I hope you have some proof of this," Pike said sharply.

Frank shook his head. "The two CIA agents I worked with are dead. Unfortunately, they left no records because of the sensitivity of the operation."

"What of General Fenton's alleged partners in these crimes? Are they available to testify?" Pike said in exasperation.

"They're all dead."

"So far, everything we heard from you resides on your credibility alone," the Senator said.

"I'm afraid so, sir."

"Doesn't the FBI have the bombing of your airliner under investigation?" Pike asked.

"Yes, sir."

"Does the FBI, as far as you know, have any evidence about what you just have been telling us?" Pike said flatly.

Frank shook his head. "No, sir, that is, outside of my personal conversation with General Fenton when he landed a helicopter on my lawn a few days ago."

Senator Pike removed his glasses and stared at Frank with an incredulous expression. "You met with General Fenton? About what?"

"He threatened to have my wife killed if I didn't withdraw my accusations. He also offered me money."

"Do you have any witnesses or documentation on this threat and bribe?" The Senator's eyes narrowed in disbelief.

"No, sir," Frank said, now somewhat frustrated.

Frank fingered the base of the microphone and paused, carefully thinking over his next words. God, I'm blowing this. Maybe if I go back to the beginning.

"Continue your story, Mister Braden," Senator Pike said

"That's about it, sir."

"Then you have no witnesses or evidence to any of your testimony?" Pike said.

"Just my word, I'm afraid."

"Mister Braden." Pike said sternly. "I hope you haven't wasted the time of myself and my fellow Senators. Outside in street are homeless transients, radicals, the insane and people with their own personal agendas, who could fabricate stories like yours and, if we accepted them without evidence, it would bring our system of government to a halt."

Frank, feeling mortified, watched the other Senators cover their mikes with their hands, nod and whisper to each other.

"We now call General Miles Fenton to testify," Pike said.

Frank left the table and sat beside Nicole.

Fenton and his attorney, a sophisticated man in his sixties, sat down at the same table Frank had vacated. Fenton moved the microphone toward him. "Senator

Pike, may I address the Senate panel on the background of my accuser?"

"Proceed."

Nicole tightened her grip around Frank's hand.

"I first met Mister Braden when I assigned him to a combat post at Marble Mountain."

"During the Vietnam War?"

"Yes, sir. I felt then he was somewhat unstable but I had hoped he would eventually recover from that. But I was sadly proven wrong when he killed his platoon commander."

Some of the Senators again whispered to each other.

"Was he charged?"

"No sir."

"Why not?" Pike said.

"He claimed self defense. I'd like to point out that he also has just admitted to you that he shot and killed another man, again claiming self-defense."

"I assume you have records on everything you're telling us?"

The general, looking very distinguished in his uniform, stood up and took several file folders from his attorney and handed them over to Senator Pike.

"Continue, general."

Fenton turned and looked at Frank with a sad expression. "It's also important to mention that after Braden landed his damaged airliner, his airline company placed him on suspension."

"What for?" Pike looked at Frank questionably.

"The FBI concluded he might be suicidal and made him their prime suspect in the bombing," Fenton said.

The general again turned and looked at Frank, shaking his head. Unseen by the Senators, Fenton gave Frank a quick smirk.

"Wouldn't look good for his airline to let a suspected suicidal captain at the controls, would it?"

Senator Pike quickly rapped his gavel on the table. "Please restrict your remarks to the facts, sir."

"My apologies, Senator. But I would like to bring out that he tried to commit suicide a second time when he recently stopped his car in the middle of the railroad tracks in the path of an Amtrak train."

Fenton turned around again and gestured toward Nicole. "I understand that if his wife hadn't come along at that time and rescued him, he would have succeeded."

"You have proof of this?" Pike demanded.

"Yes, sir. The hospital records are on your desk. In the FBI file you'll see in the remarks section that they think it was a suicide attempt."

While Pike thumbed through the files, Fenton sat down and spoke into the mike. "Braden claimed that he had been drugged, but he never even bothered to file a complaint with the local police department."

Nicole, pale, leaned to Frank. "He's twisting everything around."

Frank nodded silently. He knew that without evidence, he couldn't even give a rebuttal.

"My accuser, Frank Braden, is an unstable killer of two men and is suspected of attempting to commit suicide twice. And he has no evidence to prove any of his charges against me."

Fenton paused as his attorney leaned over and whispered into his ear.

The general stood up and looked at all the Senators as he spoke. "I stand on my record. The President of the United States has examined my background and fully approves my worthiness for the honored post of Chairman of the Joint Chiefs of Staff."

Senator Pike looked at his watch. "Panel will adjourn for lunch. We will start hearing witnesses at two o'clock."

Frank and Nicole walked hand in hand slowly out of the Senate hearing room. Frank, looking defeated, had his head down, his mind in deep thought. Nicole noticed that everyone in the room watched them leave but avoided eye contact.

17

In the Senate lunchroom Frank and Nicole sat alone at a table. Frank's mood was somber, having barely said more than five words since they left the hearing. Around them the lively conversations and joviality at the surrounding tables were quite noticeable.

Nicole decided to break the silence. "I'm glad that none of this will be made public. They're making you out to be a—."

"A suicidal fool?"

Nicole grabbed his hand. "I'm sorry, I didn't mean it to come out that way." She bent her head down and started to sob softly.

"Doesn't matter anymore. The damage has been done."

Nicole lifts her wet eyes, puzzled. "What do you mean? No reporters were allowed at the hearing."

"Bill Bellman from our front office was at the hearing this morning. He's a witness for Fenton."

"Oh, Frank," Nicole said softly.

"My flying days for WestSky or for anyone else are over."

Distraught, Nicole dropped her fork with a loud clank on the side of her salad plate, drawing stares from nearby

Senators who attended the hearing. Her expression became bitter. "My God, the bad guy is winning, isn't he?"

Frank nodded. "I got to come up with something this afternoon or it'll be all over."

"There must be somebody alive in this world who knows about Fenton," Nicole said determinedly.

Frank stopped eating his sandwich in mid-bite. "Nicole, you just may have hit the jackpot."

Nicole looked confused as Frank quickly stood up and grabbed her hand. He reached for the check and pulled Nicole up and motioned for her to follow him from the lunchroom. "Let's go. I've got to see the CIA at Langley."

18

Frank and Nicole arrived back at the hearing room fifteen minutes late for the start of the afternoon session. A WestSky Airlines executive was sitting patiently at the witness table. Senator Pike glared at them as they took their seats but said nothing.

Senator Pike rapped his gavel down hard, startling a few Senators who were conferring with their aides. "This hearing is now in session." He looked down at the witness. "State your name and occupation, please."

"William Bellman. Director of Personnel for WestSky Airlines," he said. A big, solid man with flecks of gray in his hair, he had a commanding presence in his dark blue suit and red tie.

"Do you know Frank Braden?"

"Yes sir."

Senator Pike shifted uncomfortably in his seat and exchanged glances with Frank. "What's your opinion of his mental condition?"

"I can't say from a personal opinion nor am I qualified as a physician or therapist, but I can give you the view of our company."

"And that is?"

"Currently, Mister Braden is temporary suspended from all flying duties pending the outcome of the FBI investigation."

"Why is that, sir?"

"At the start of the investigation, the FBI informed us that they suspected that Mister Braden planted the bomb himself to commit suicide. And until that is proven or disproved, Mister Braden will remain on suspension," Bellman said firmly.

"Do you have anything further to add?"

"Upon hearing about a second alleged suicide attempt, I personally don't think Mister Braden will be flying with us any longer."

A parade of military officers from captains to Generals took the witness stand the rest of that afternoon, praising the worthiness of General Fenton to assume the office of Chairman of the Joint Chiefs of Staff.

After the last witness for General Fenton finished his testimony, the senators again conferred among themselves. After a few minutes, Senator Pike returned to his microphone. "Mister Braden, this is your last chance. Do you have any witnesses to present at this hearing?"

Frank walked to the table, sat down and fingered the microphone. "Sir, I have just learned of the existence of a witness who can support my allegations."

In the rear seats, Fenton's attorney looked at the general questionably. Fenton smirked and shook his head. The senators became strangely quiet as they stared at Frank.

"Are you prepared to call him now?" Pike said.

"No sir, not at the moment." Frank fiddled with the mike before looking up. "Since today is Friday, I would like to ask that this hearing be postponed until next Thursday to allow me to bring my witness here."

The lawyer for Fenton jumped to his feet. "Mister Chairman, my client has suffered enough humiliation at this man's unfounded allegations. Is he going to need this time to look for a witness in the mental institutions? It would be unfair to my client to have this hearing extended for another six days."

The Senators conferred among themselves, most shaking their heads. Pike stayed in front of his microphone, somewhat aloof from the others while he pondered both requests.

"Are you sure this witness's testimony will be relevant?" Pike said sternly.

"Yes sir."

Pike covered his mike and conferred with his colleagues. After a minute, the Senators returned to their seats. Pike rapped his gavel. "Considering the important nature of this hearing, we will adjourn until Thursday morning at ten when Mister Braden may present his witness."

19

Three days later, Frank and Nicole were in their living room. Frank held the newspaper in front of his face and Nicole was knitting furiously. Both appeared so intent on their activities that it was obvious their minds were elsewhere.

Nicole broke the silence first. "Didn't they say they would phone you this afternoon?"

"Or tomorrow morning or never," Frank said. "The CIA is funny that way if they don't want to get involved."

"What if he says no?"

"That's simple. I'll call Senator Pike to cancel Thursday and then apply for cooking school or perhaps take a plumbing course."

"Silly," Nicole replied.

The doorbell rang and both of them instantly looked at the phone before realizing their mistake. Nicole went to the front door. "I'll be glad when these next few days are history."

A man in a brown UPS uniform smiled when Nicole opened the door and handed her a package, clipboard and pen. "Please sign here ma'am."

Nicole took the package into the kitchen and with a knife cut the strings around the container.

"Who was that?" Frank said from the living room.

"UPS. I got a package."

"Who from?"

Nicole stopped and looked at the sender's address. "From a P. Burnside." She cut the last string and removed the wrapping.

As Nicole attempted to pull the top cover off the box, Frank ran in and hit her hands hard, knocking them away from the package. "Don't," he yelled.

Nicole, with a startled look on her face, rubbed her wrist where Frank had hit her. "Addressed to me," she said defensively.

"Fenton sent it,"

"Don't go paranoid on me," Nicole said.

Frank looked at the wrapping and pointed to the return address. "P. Burnside means Pat Burnside, my brother's old CIA alias."

Nicole, bewildered, backed away from the table. "What should we do?"

Frank eyed the package suspiciously. "Since it didn't explode bouncing around in that UPS truck, I think I can hold it." He gently lifted the package and carried it out the rear door.

Frank gently carried the box halfway down to the lake. He glanced back and looked satisfied that he was far enough away to avoid damage to his home. As Nicole watched from a safe distance, he carefully placed it on the lawn.

"Should we call the police?" Nicole said.

"I'm not sure."

"Why not? Don't you think it a bomb, anymore?"

Frank circled the container while he studied it. "Why would he try to harm you in the middle of the hearings? He'd only defeat himself."

"Because he's mad, he's a nut, whatever. I don't care. Call the damn police," Nicole could feel the tension rising inside her.

Frank knelt down and looked closely at the box. "If it's not a bomb and I call the cops, I would look paranoid. And I'm sure Fenton would alert the Senators to this."

Frank got up and walked back to the garage. He returned with a long metal pole. He pushed a nearby redwood picnic table over and got behind it. "Go in the house. I think I'll be safe here."

"No. I'm not going to let you do this. I'm calling the police," Nicole said in a panic-stricken voice.

Frank, breathing hard now, edged the pole towards the lid of the box. "Don't bother. If it's a bomb, they'll hear."

Nicole gasped and ran toward the house as Frank positioned the pole under the tip of the lid. When he heard the rear screen door slam he scrunched his face as he gently lifted the lid off the box. To his surprise it fell off easily, no levers or springs attached to it. "Put down the phone, Nicole, it's a fake," he yelled in relief.

Nicole came cautiously out the door. Frank got up and leaned over the container to look inside. A typed note lay on the bottom of the box. He picked the paper up and read it.

"Jesus!" Frank shouted. He dropped the note and dashed past Nicole to the house.

Nicole apprehensively picked up the note and read the frightening words, "Sorry, I forgot to enclose your gift. But I didn't forget the gifts for your kids, Susan and Richard."

She screamed, dropped the note and ran toward the house.

20

General Fenton sat in his cushioned chair looking across his desk at his attorney.

"What is the necessity of having this meeting, counsel? Aren't we making a big enough fool out of my accuser?"

"I want to make sure it continues that way," the attorney said dryly. He took out a notepad and pencil. "Now, you tell me all the possible names of a witness that Braden could come up with. I want no surprises."

Fenton shrugged. "If I knew, that person would never make it to the hearing."

"I didn't hear that," the attorney replied.

"What I meant was that nobody is still alive who could disprove or confirm his accusations. They're dead. It's a simple as that," Fenton said, displaying an attitude varying between confidence and boredom.

"There must be something, somebody out there," the attorney persisted. "As much as a fool we made Braden appear, he led me, and apparently Senator Pike, to believe that this witness will show. Braden seems determined to prove that you are guilty of his accusations. In short, I don't think he's bluffing."

"Careful, counsel, you seem to be taking his side," Fenton glared.

"I got to play the devil's advocate to avoid any surprises."

Fenton's secretary came on the intercom. "General, you have a call on your private number. It's a man and he wouldn't give me his name. He said to tell you that the packages were delivered."

"Put him on hold." The general looked at the attorney. "Tell you what. I'm going to think very hard about who this witness could be. If I come up with anything I'll call you at your office." Fenton stood up and held out his hand. "Thanks for your concern."

The attorney looked nonplussed. "I really wanted to settle this matter now, if you—."

"Good day and thanks for coming," the general interrupted.

The attorney left without another word. As soon as the man left the office, Fenton picked up his phone. "Delivery went okay?"

"I couldn't be in two places at once but I was on campus when UPS delivered them to the two students. Those are the important packages, anyway, right?"

"I'd say they could generate some interest in that particular household. Yes," Fenton said with a half smile. "Look, I may need you for a particular job. I'll contact you when I get a name."

21

Frank rapidly tapped his fingers against the countertop as he held the phone to his ear. "Oh God. Answer. Answer, please."

Nicole ran into the kitchen and Frank pointed a finger to a cell phone lying on the counter. "Call the campus police and tell them to get over to Susan's and Richard's dorms. Tell 'em that they might have gotten a package bomb." Frank was sweating as he waited for someone to answer the phone.

Nicole, breathing hard, dialed the cell phone. "Operator, put me through to the campus police, hurry," she almost screamed into the phone.

"Hello?" A young man's voice came over Frank's earphone.

Frank sighed in relief. "Richard. If you get a package, don't open it! Run to Susan's dorm, and tell her the same. We think—"

"Calm down, dad. The only package I got was from a P. Burnside."

"Don't open it," Frank said quickly.

"Cool it, dad. It was addressed to me. I opened it. Susan did, too."

124

"Anything in it?" Frank spoke more calmly now. He motioned to Nicole to stop her phone call.

"You bet," Richard said. We both got twenty-dollar bills. A note said to live it up and have a few beers on him. What relative is he, dad?"

Frank took a deep breath and gave Nicole a thumbs up sign. She placed the cell phone down. "He's no relative. Now listen carefully. Don't you and Susan open any more unexpected packages you get in the mail or by a delivery service. I think someone is trying to hurt members of our family. I'll give you more details later."

Nicole walked to Frank's side and held out her hand for the phone.

Frank whispered to Nicole. "Fenton is letting us know he can reach any of us." He handed the phone to her. She started crying as she talked to her son.

22

Later that same afternoon, Nicole resumed her knitting but again it was obvious that her mind was elsewhere. Suddenly, in a fit of anger, she threw the knitting to the floor and glared at Frank.

"I swore on my oath as a physician to save lives. But I swear that I will personally and physically destroy this damn General if he hurts one of my children."

Frank pulled down the newspaper from his face that he hadn't been reading and calmly replied, "Not if I get to him first."

"I'm so upset and confused by all of this I just don't know what to do." Nicole stammered. "For instance, I never even knew that you killed the man who shot you in Vietnam until the General brought it up at the hearing. What is the story on that?"

"He was a phony CIA agent that I trusted. I first got to know him intimately when we were flying a planeload of boxes from Vientiane to Da Nang. Before the flight I secretly opened one of the boxes and discovered it contained bags of heroin. My co-pilot was our new platoon commander, a captain named Wenzel.

"When I tried to radio ahead to have the MPs meet the plane, he turned off my radio so I pulled my Army issued .45-caliber pistol on him. But in one of the slickest maneuvers I ever saw, he nearly blinded me with his fingers and twisted the gun away from me. He could've shot me but instead he claimed to be an undercover agent sent to the unit by the CIA to keep a protective eye on me. He said that the shipment we carried was being monitored by the CIA to learn its final destination and for me not to interfere. But all the time he was a silent partner with Fenton. He had me fooled.

"Actually, it was Lan who later alerted me to a silent partner. This occurred during my last flight to Vientiane when I was sent to search for Parker's plane. Parker had disappeared enroute to Da Nang in a sabotaged plane that I was supposed to fly. After landing at the Vientiane airport I couldn't find any members of our unit who were stationed there. At the time I was unaware that Lan was having them murdered because of a mistaken double-cross until I walked into his nightclub and saw him sitting calmly at that same table."

I stopped just inside the entrance of the ballroom when I saw two Lao detectives standing next to Lan who sat with his usual cup of tea. From the high pitched tone of their voices the Laotians appeared to be issuing an ultimatum to Lan. The senior investigator flipped a passport onto the table as the detectives headed for the door.

This time I approached Lan with a little more caution.

"Ah yes, Mister Braden, I thought I might see you one last time."

"One last time? That shouldn't surprise me. You seem to be in trouble with just about everybody including the local authorities. Did they inquire about Suzi's death that you ordered?"

"I did not order Suzi's death," Lan said defensively. "She was like the daughter I wished I had."

"Then who killed her?"

"I am afraid the death was ordered by members of my organization. I could not prevent them."

"You mean the Vietcong, don't you?"

"Ah, you have become aware of that."

"Is that why the Laotians are kicking you out?"

"One reason," Lan said calmly as if discussing an unimportant business matter. "There was also the problem of the Laotian bodies of the four assassins your people sent to dispose of me. That is when the police began to suspect that I had too many connections."

"My people?"

"Perhaps not exactly your people. But the people you have been sent to investigate."

"You know about that?"

"We have our ways." He motioned for me to sit down. "It is not very often I get to talk to an enemy soldier who is aware of who I am without trying to kill him."

I sat down warily. I felt uncomfortable since I wasn't too sure of Lan's intentions. So, I lifted up the right side of my fatigue shirt revealing that I carried the .45 sidearm.

Lan did not fail to take notice. "Before you get any pretentious ideas, Mister Braden, I think you remember that I carry a Chicom pistol in my pocket and I, unlike you pilots, am a very good shot."

"It's only for defensive purposes," I said, not taking his eyes off my adversary. "And I'll be the first to admit that I probably could do more damage by throwing it at you. Then again, I could get off a lucky shot."

The comment caused Lan to relax and he leaned back in his chair. "I just wanted to remind you that we are both in neutral territory and we must respect that."

I glanced at my watch. "Sorry, but I can't stay long to discuss our philosophies," I said rising. "I'm in the middle of a serial search for Parker."

"Oh yes, Parker." Lan shook his head. "I'm afraid that he took the plane that you were supposed to fly. You see, they were onto you also. They rigged the aircraft. Whoever flew it was not supposed to reach their destination."

I sat back down. "That means Parker was not a part of the smuggling ring."

"But, ah, he was. The others did not tell him they had planned to kill you because they were afraid that he would not go along with it. Unknowingly, he took your flight. And he became a victim of fortune."

"Why did they try to kill you?" I asked, trying to put all the pieces of the puzzle together from the man who seemed to know it all.

"They no longer needed me."

"Who?"

"Your American smugglers. They have also gone to their fortunes."

"Dead?"

"Almost all are or soon will be," Lan said. "I do not take betrayal lightly."

"You mean the Bobbsey twins and Butterworth?"

"And others."

"You know I will inform the local police and have you arrested."

"Report me? For getting rid of your trash? You should thank me." Lan shook his head. "I would be in the North Vietnamese Embassy before they got the courage to arrest me. They are not too eager to upset local diplomatic relations with the North Vietnamese and the Pathet Lao."

I glanced again at my watch. "Now that we have agreed on non-agreement, I have an air search to conduct."

I got out of the chair, never taking my eyes off Lan, and backed away several meters before turning around and walked toward the door.

"Mister Braden. I would advise you to watch your back better than that."

I stopped and turned. "Did you think of shooting me?"

"No," Lan smiled. "There is another silent partner among the smugglers that you are not aware of. I suspect that he will try to kill you since you are the main witness against his group."

"Who's that?"

"I would prefer not to tell you," Lan said, looking thoughtfully into his teacup. "I would prefer that one of you kill the other. That would make one less enemy in my country."

"You didn't any have idea who he might have been talking about?" Nicole said.

"Not at that time." Frank said. "There were too many possibilities. For instance, there was Major Clements. After all, the First Sergeant and the Executive Officer were part of the smugglers, so why not the Major? Then again, it could have been another crewchief or sergeant or pilot or maybe someone in Battalion. I decided to suspect everyone for my own safety. I even had doubts about Captain Wenzel who claimed to be a CIA agent put there to protect me. Good thing, too."

"Who are the Bobbsey twins? Are they really twins?" Nicole asked.

"I had to ask that same question when I first heard about them," Frank smiled. "Their names were Buddy Brooks and Ralph Asher. They were called the Bobbsey twins because they always flew together and they were the only pilots from our unit stationed in Laos. Usually, in Vietnam, unit pilots switch off with each other but since they were alone in Vientiane, and for the very good reason of keeping their smuggling operation secret, they only flew the CIA covert missions over there. They had extended their tours and were there nearly two years."

"What were they like?"

Frank shrugged. "I guess the description for them would be, standoffish, secretive.

They would never pass for twins, Buddy stretched to a hulking 6-foot-5 and Ralph resembled a sawed off California redwood, stout around the girth but stood no more than 5-foot-5."

"Who was this Butterworth?"

"Their crewchief. He also extended his tour with them. Of course, he was involved in the smuggling, too."

"What was he like?"

"I would best describe him as slimy. Every time he shook my hand, I felt like I needed to take a shower."

"So what happened?"

"The VC guys who planted the bomb set it off under the fuel storage tank." Frank said. "By the time the crash trucks from the airfield arrived, there was a wall of fire where the barracks and storage tank once stood."

"Did they catch them?" Nicole asked.

"Who?"

"Those Viet Cong who set off the blast."

"Oh no. They're too quick, too experienced in retreating through the underbrush. It took a while for the American investigators to even determine what caused the fuel tank to explode. When I made my landing approach hours later on that same day from the sea to runway three zero at Nha Trang, I had been watching the column of black smoke rising from the fuel storage tank from twenty miles out."

"Did you know then what had happened?"

"No, but I knew it wouldn't be good," Frank said. "You see, to a pilot, black smoke usually meant an oil based fire, possibly from an aircraft accident."

23

I landed and after parking the Otter, I headed for the orderly room, hoping to find Wenzel, Major Clements and perhaps CIA agents waiting for me. I figured all the cards were out on the table now and it was time to bring the remaining criminals to light.

It was a few minutes after five in the afternoon and the clerks had already taken off when I entered the building.

"I figured you'd be here about this time," came a voice from the commander's office. Captain Wenzel, taking a cigar from his lips, got up out of the major's chair and walked over and held out his hand. He wore civilian calfskin black flying boots and slacks of the same color. A Yankees baseball cap covered his head. I wondered if he traded his Army uniform in for a regular spook outfit.

"Congratulations," Wenzel said as we shook hands. "You broke up the ring."

"They sabotaged Tom's plane," I said in an urgent voice. "He's out there somewhere. We got to offer a leniency deal to one of those involved to find out what they did to the plane. Then maybe we can pinpoint Tom's location."

"Did you see that smoke as you landed?" Wenzel interrupted.

"Yeah. What's it from?"

Wenzel took a deep drag on his cigar and watched the smoke curl up toward the ceiling. "It's probably from what's left of Fenton, Clyde and Wilson."

"Come again?"

"They were in Fenton's room when the storage tank blew. Probably never knew what hit them. Fortunately or unfortunately, however you might put it, they were the only ones in the officer's barracks at that time."

"This has to be Lan's work," I said glumly. Assuming that Parker was no longer alive, seven of the group had died within a day of each other.

"I agree, it probably was Lan," Wenzel said.

"Where's the major?"

"Left on a C130 for Saigon shortly before the blast. We called him. He'll be back tomorrow."

"Does he know about the smuggling ring?"

"No. We want to check him out a little bit more before we tell him what's going on." Wenzel took another puff on his cigar and eyed me curiously. He seemed to be waiting for a specific question.

"Are the other CIA people around?"

"I thought you would never ask. We're meeting them in a few minutes. Come on, I'll drive." Wenzel started for the door.

I propped my right boot on the metal frame of the jeep as Wenzel drove past the base entrance toward town. I looked over at Wenzel. "Why didn't they come on base?"

"They like to stay out of the limelight. How long has it been you last saw them?"

"A month or two. I'm beginning to feel like a veteran. By the way, I forgot their names. What are they?" I asked.

"I dunno. They got agents coming in and out of the country all the time."

The jeep proceeded deeper into the heart of the city. As we drove around a three-foot high circular cement monument in the center of a multi street intersection, the smelly fermented fish sauce of nuoc mam permeated the air. Wenzel, cigar clenched in his teeth, weaved around and through the multitudes of taxis and Lambretta motor scooters and bikes.

"From what you told the flight operations specialist, you must've talked to Lan?" Wenzel said.

"Sure did."

"Why did he kill them?"

"He believed they had sent assassins to kill him," I said.

"What else did he tell you?"

"Not much." I hesitated to tell Wenzel about the silent partner. I figured I'd wait and drop that bomb in front of the other CIA agents.

"Ah, here we are," Wenzel said as he turned down a narrow street leading to a cluster of apartments on the second and third floors above a motorbike repair shop. He pulled the jeep next to an alley and turned off the motor.

"Will the jeep be safe here?" I said looking around.

"Now it will be." Wenzel reached down and brought up a chain and paddock that he slipped around the steering wheel. "You're right about this being out in nowhere city. There are still terrorists around here. Got ammo for your forty-five?" He eyed my pistol's empty butt handle hanging in my holster.

I shrugged. "No. I left the ammo clip in the aircraft. Base regulations, remember? No loaded weapon for transient pilots. You got one?"

"Nope. Never carried one except in combat," Wenzel replied. "Spooks know how to use knives, hands and feet. They know it's just as effective."

I followed Wenzel through a deserted alley and up the stairs to a door on the third floor, the only apartment atop the concrete building.

Wenzel stopped and knocked rapidly four times, pausing a second before hitting the door a fifth time. He shrugged his shoulders. "They're not here, yet." He reached inside his pocket and brought out a key. "This is one of their cover houses."

Inside, the room had no windows. The pale yellow of its thick cement walls and gray concrete floor, made the interior look like a prison cell. A plain wood table with two chairs sat in the middle of the room. Wenzel closed the heavy door with a thud and turned on the sole light bulb dangling from the ceiling.

"I like it because it's nearly soundproof," Wenzel commented. "I personally rented it and told the gook leasing it that I was a worker employed by one of the American construction companies. Paid him in full for a year. That was several months ago, I don't think he'll ever remember me. To them all Americans look alike."

I looked around and didn't like the setup one bit. I had begun to feel uneasy ever since we were traveling in the jeep. I figured I had nothing to lose now by calling Wenzel's bluff. "You're no damn CIA agent, are you?"

"So, you finally caught on. Or did Lan tell you?" Wenzel turned and locked the door from the inside and put the key in his pocket. "Either way, it's a little bit too late."

"If Lan had told me outright, I wouldn't be here now."

"So how did you know?"

"You used the term 'they' too many times today when describing how spooks operate. It should've been 'we.' That was my second hint. The third came when I saw this room minus any CIA agents. But the first warning sign came when you didn't know the names of Chuck and Al. How could you help protect me when only they knew the details of my covert assignment."

"Clever."

"So you think you can take me with just your hands and feet," I challenged. *God I hope he's not that tough or I'm in deep trouble.*

"Not really." Wenzel casually reached down and pulled out a snub-nosed .38 caliber revolver from a tiny holster clipped to the inside of his right boot. He then reached inside a pocket and brought out a noise suppressor tube that he attached to the gun barrel.

I watched with a sense of detached curiosity, like it was a dream sequence rather than reality. My only reaction was to pull out my Army issued pistol. The heaviness of the gun made it as dangerous as a blackjack.

"I thought you said you were not armed," I said.

"I lied."

Wenzel held the revolver casually, tapping the extended barrel in the palm of his left hand, as though he was ready to offer me a deal I couldn't refuse. His eyes narrowed like a cat, toying with a cornered mouse. "Now there's two ways we can do this. Messy and painful with many shots or you can turn around and take one quick shot into the brain."

I was sweating, knowing that these moments could be my last. "There's something you should know." I raised my forty-five and pointed it at Wenzel. "We got a Mexican standoff."

"What?"

"You see, I chambered a round before I withdrew the clip."

Wenzel smiled. "Expect me to fall for that bull, chief?" He pulled the hammer back on his revolver and pointed it at my head.

I pulled the hammer back on my forty-five and pointed the weapon at Wenzel's chest. With the table between us, I moved to his left to throw off Wenzel's aim.

A look of doubt now crossed Wenzel's face and he moved to his right and lowered his revolver at an easier target — my chest.

We circled the room, pistols pointed, eyeing each other like two fighting dogs in a pit, waiting for the slightest motion from the other to attack.

I saw a tightening of muscles in Wenzel's gun hand and I squeezed my trigger. Both guns fired simultaneously.

A force spun me around and down, blood from my upper left chest started soaking through my uniform.

Wenzel took my forty-five's big slug squarely in the chest and his body slammed hard against the wall as though a large spike had been driven through him. Wordlessly, he slumped down to the floor with a shocked expression forever frozen on his face.

"Did you ever think of what would have happened if you had missed on your single shot?" Nicole said.

"I wouldn't be here with you now."

"Except for Fenton, all members of the smuggling ring died a violent death," Nicole pointed out. "How many did Lan kill?"

"Under his orders there were three killed in Vientiane. Buddy, Ralph and Charley. Three in Nha Trang but actually only two in Nha Trang since Fenton escaped. I shot Wenzel and Parker was dispatched accidentally by his own smugglers."

Nicole counted on her fingers. "So there were eight smugglers in the group, total."

"That's right."

"So, that's eight out of how many personnel in your company?"

"About 196 men and officers."

"That meant about four percent of your company were crooks."

"I prefer to think of it as ninety-six percent of our company were honest men. And that's a better percentage of honest men than you'll ever find in our civilian community."

"What about the two CIA agents who got you into this mess?"

"I did have one farewell meeting with them."

Like ghosts from the past, CIA agents Chuck and Al sat in Major Clements' office when I entered wearing a stateside uniform, with my arm in a cast.

It had been a long three days since I had phoned the Group S2 office in Saigon to report that I needed to contact the CIA. At first, Group didn't know my connection to the CIA and needed some convincing.

The events of the last month had unraveled so fast that even I had begun to worry if my CIA contacts were legit.

So it was with some relief that I stood facing the men seated before me. Chuck was the first to speak. "In all honesty we never thought you'd be this good."

The other agent chipped in, "There's nobody left alive."

"I only defended myself," I protested. "Lan did the rest."

"Any way you look at it, you took the agency off the hook. More important to us, it precludes the necessity of a trial," Chuck said.

"And the accompanying publicity," Al injected. "Now we won't have to face Congress."

"Is the mission finished in Laos?"

"Yep, Commies know too much about it now." Chuck answered.

"What about Lan?"

"You would have batted a thousand if you could've gotten rid of him, too," Al grinned. "By the time we got the Laos intelligence people to go after him, he had left the country aboard a North Vietnamese Embassy flight to Hanoi. I suspect he'll soon be back operating in the III Corps boonies."

"You know," I said, "he firmly believes that his side will outlast us."

"The way we are fighting this damn war, he might just be right," Chuck said grimly.

"Going back to the frigging States for treatment?" Al said, nodding at my bandages.

"Frigging?" I questioned.

Chuck laughed. " He has been here too long. We'd been ordered to reprogram his language."

Al nodded. "Last time I was in Washington I had lunch with our director and his wife. She turned different shades of blue every time I spoke."

I laughed and looked at my watch. It was getting close to departure time for a plane I didn't want to miss. I shook hands with the two agents and headed for the door.

"Keep in touch," Chuck said with a wink.

I shook my head. "Like hell I will."

❖ ❖ ❖

Frank glanced up at Nicole whose eyes were riveted on him. "That was nearly thirty years ago."

"That's the last time I ever saw them alive. I guess they died in a helicopter crash the day after I went back to the States."

"Sounds like an adventure novel," she said.

"I wish it were."

"Except for the part where I treated you at the Great Lakes Naval Hospital."

"Yep, that's right. Without that gunshot wound, I'd still be a happy bachelor," Frank teased.

"Wrong. You'd just be a bachelor." She pulled him over and kissed him before pushing him away playfully.

"What type of plane did they haul these poppies in?" Nicole asked.

"I like to think of it as an escapee from the Smithsonian Institute. The aircraft was an eleven-seat de Havilland Otter. The Army termed it a U-1A. The letter U is for utility. Basically, it was the largest single-engine passenger plane on this side of the old Iron Curtain. It had a solitary, radial engine of 600 horsepower bolted to the nose that pulled the high-wing plane slowly through the air, resembling a caricature of the monoplanes that shared the sky in the thirties. It was a tail dragger and its wings and fuselage are best described as fat and it wasn't too fast. About 130 miles-per-hour. But it could fly a big load slowly into a tiny 700-foot long rough field. I loved flying it."

Nicole looked puzzled. "If it's that awkward and slow why did they use it for a secret mission?"

Frank raised a finger to emphasize his next point. "With the throttle pulled back these three-bladed Otters are almost noiseless in a glide."

"So?"

"Had a great glide ratio. Starting a glide from 10,000 feet, the Otter can move smoothly, silently downward for several miles to the target area. At night, over an enemy jungle encampment without radar, they are practically invisible. This allowed a squad of Nungs to parachute out near the encampment without fear of detection."

"Nungs?"

"These are professional mercenaries paid by us to kill or capture VC and North Vietnam military leaders in their sanctuaries in Laos and Cambodia. They wear the uniform of the enemy. They speak the language and they look like the enemy. The Nungs migrated into Vietnam from the Indo-China border area. They've been mercenary fighters for centuries. It's their trade."

"I do remember reading something about this in Time or Newsweek back in the seventies when I was in college," Nicole said.

"Yep, the 'Dragnet' story broke in the news media around the mid-to-late seventies," Frank said. "This was the covert mission that the two CIA agents were trying to protect. I understand it was very successful and didn't allow enemy commanders to feel safe even in their safest border sanctuaries. Unfortunately, when the Bobbsey twins weren't flying these 'Dragnet' missions, they were out hauling poppies from the isolated Laotian villages. The plane could land on unimproved jungle strips next to these villages."

24

Inside the Senate hearing room members of the panel take their seats as ten o'clock approached. Frank was already seated at the witness table and Nicole sat behind him. He kept looking over his shoulder as if he were expecting someone. Exactly on the hour, Senator Pike arrived and assumed his chairman position in front of Frank.

Pike rapped his gavel on the table as he quickly assessed the area around Frank. It was apparent he wasn't impressed with what he saw and a scowl wrinkled the lines in his face. "This hearing is now convened," Pike said, brushing away a flock of silver hair that had fallen on his forehead. "Mister Braden? Are you ready to present your witness?"

"No sir. He isn't here," Frank said grimly. *And I don't know where he is or if he's even coming.*

"Mister Braden, we've adjourned for six days in order for you to present a witness at ten this morning. What part of that didn't you understand?" Since Pike had gone out on a limb in front of his fellow Senators to allow postponement of the hearing, he was quite displeased over Frank's failure to present a witness.

"I understand, sir. But we need more time. The witness is coming from overseas," Frank pleaded.

"Has he arrived in this country, yet?"

"Frankly, I don't know. I haven't been able to get hold of the CIA personnel who have been assisting me in obtaining the witness."

Felton's attorney stood up. "Sir. My client objects to any more delays for his confirmation. I think everyone here agrees that he has suffered enough humiliation from this malicious gossip."

The others Senators looked at their chairman and nodded their heads. Senator Pike accepted their consensus and rapped his gavel again on the table. "I'm inclined to agree with the counselor for General Fenton. This hearing is—."

At that moment, the doors in the rear opened and an elderly man walked slowly down the aisle. He wore a dark suit and with one glance took in the whole assembly. He smiled when he saw General Fenton.

Frank stood up and waved the man to his table. "Sir, my witness has arrived." Frank said with a twinkle in his eyes. Frank then moved away from his table, sat down next to Nicole and put his arm around her shoulder and gave her a triumphal squeeze. Nicole couldn't take her eyes off the man proceeding down the aisle.

General Fenton's heart started beating faster and his face turned a chalky white as he ignored questions from his attorney. Jesus, why didn't I think of him, he told himself.

Senator rapped his gavel for quiet as he eyed the witness. "Your name and occupation, sir?"

"I am Binh Lan, Minister of Education of the Socialist Republic of Vietnam," he said. Lan sat in front of the mike, his hands linked on the table, calmly waiting for the next question.

The Senators glanced at each other and then focused their attention on the witness. General Fenton sat immobilized as he continued to ignore whispered questions from his now frantic attorney.

"May I see your credentials and passport, please?" Pike said.

Lan rose and walked over to Senator Pike and presented his papers. He then returned to his seat.

"Sir, are you acquainted with General Fenton?" Pike began his questioning cautiously.

Lan's smile broadened and he turned in his seat and looked at the general. "Yes. Captain Fenton and I were business partners."

"What kind of business, sir?"

"In my primary business I was a Colonel in command of several Viet Cong battalions in the Saigon sector. I also operated a bar and house of prostitution in Vientiane, Laos, called Lannie's."

Fenton slinked lower in his chair, still ignoring questions from his attorney.

"I see," Pike said, trying to avoid the appearance of a judgmental attitude. "And what type of business did you have with the then Captain Fenton?"

"You might say we were . . . in the transportation business."

"Exactly what did you transport?" Pike said impatiently.

"I would arrange with Melo farmers to buy their poppy crops and Captain Fenton would supply his Army planes to fly the opium out of the villages to a Corsican processing lab in Vientiane."

"I see," Pike said, "and then what happened at the lab?"

"The poppies would be processed into heroin," Lan

said. "Some of the heroin would be taken back to Vietnam aboard his Army planes for distribution."

"Sold to our troops?" Pike said angrily.

"They were my main customers for obvious reasons," Lan said. "But the Corsicans also would distribute it to their markets in France, Hong Kong and the United States."

Senator Pike realized that he was addressing a very cunning former enemy commander and he resolved not to let his anger show over a war fought thirty years ago. So he switched subjects. "Did the then Captain Fenton have anything to do with the murder of Mister Braden's brother?

"If you are referring to a CID operative by the name of Burnside, yes. Unknown to them, I witnessed the event."

"Did they tell you explicitly that they were going to kill this man?" Pike said.

"Not explicitly," Lan explained. "You see I am the one who told them that Burnside was working for the CIA. Our agents in Saigon informed me of this fact. I knew by their reaction what was going to happen. I expected it and we secretly watched it."

"Watched?" Pike repeated.

Lan smiled. "Yes, we knew we would always have Captain Fenton in our power if we held incriminating evidence against him."

Frank glared at Lan with mixed feelings. Here was this man willing to come ten thousand miles to get Fenton indicted for the murder of his brother, and other crimes, Frank told himself, and yet, he was the one who tipped off the smugglers that led to his brother's death.

"So you are what we term an accessory to the murder," Pike said sternly.

"Not exactly. You must remember that it was wartime and all Americans soldiers were my enemy. It was simply a matter of eliminating one and using this information for possible blackmail later." Lan then turned around and looked at Frank with a sad expression. "I am sorry but at the time I did not know it was your brother. But to be honest, it would not have made a difference. I think, as a soldier, you will understand that."

Fenton sat in the rear frozen to his seat, his face drained of color, still avoiding the plea of his attorney for answers to his questions.

"Did you witness this murder yourself?" Pike said.

"Yes."

"Can you give us the details?"

"Yes. We heard from our agent, a barracks' maid in Nha Trang, that they planned to kill Burnside at the spot where their company dumped their used aviation oil.

I remember it was raining as I arrived before them and I crouched down in the elephant grass. Soon Captain Fenton and Sergeant Wilson drove up and parked the jeep back in the jungle. Sergeant Wilson climbed out and hid himself in the foliage several yards away from the oil pit while Captain Fenton stayed in his covered jeep. When the soldier called Burnside arrived, Sergeant Wilson shot him. Both he and Captain Fenton dumped the body into the oil pit."

There was a noticeable silence inside the hearing room. Frank sat stunned, feeling sick to his stomach. Nicole clutched his arm, trying to give him comfort and support.

Senator Pike cleared his throat. "Go on, Mister Lan."

"Fenton walked to his jeep and both vehicles left the area," Lan said. "They were probably comforted by the knowledge that Vietnam with its daily reports of missing men had put the odds in their favor to get away with murder."

"Any more on this murder?" Pike said.

"The next time I met Captain Fenton he bragged to me that he waited three days before he typed a report listing SP4 Pat Burnside as AWOL to battalion head-quarters," Lan said,

Fenton elbowed his lawyer and the attorney leaped to his feet. "I object. This witness admitted he's a drug smuggler, pimp and enemy soldier. He's also a liar. Where's his proof? He obviously is prejudiced toward American heroes who served in Vietnam."

Senator Pike rapped his gavel on the table twice. "Please remain in your seat, counselor."

Nicole had to physically restrain Frank from rising from his chair. He stared hard at Fenton and Frank's lips formed the words, 'You lying bastard.'

Lan looked over at Fenton and smiled.

Senator Pike calmly continued his questioning. "This whole affair is an incredible story, sir, and several things seem illogical. For one, how could you command your battalions in Vietnam while running a bar in Laos?"

Lan turned around again and looked at Fenton and held up a finger as if to indicate the best is yet to come. "Captain Fenton's Army planes flew me between Laos and Vietnam many times."

"Didn't the South Vietnam custom agents get suspicious of all this travel on your passport?"

"I never needed a passport. Vietnamese customs would never check U.S. military planes. Thanks to

Captain Fenton, I was able to get to Saigon before TET to lead my troops in battle."

Some of the Senators gasped as they glared at Fenton.

"Did General, er, Captain Fenton know that you were a VC?" Senator Pike asked.

"It would not have been to my advantage to let him know."

"Why are you testifying against General Fenton now?"

"Because until a few days ago, I did not know he was alive," Lan said firmly. "He tried to have me assassinated back then and I have a long memory."

Senator Pike reviewed some of the notes he had been making. "All we have now is your testimony. Do you have any visible evidence in support of your accusations?"

Fenton looked at his attorney with a sense of relief. "Believe me, everything he said is all hogwash. He doesn't have any proof because there is none. He's simply a Vietnamese agent trying to screw up the President's appointment of me as Chief of Staff. For what devious reason I couldn't guess."

The attorney studied Fenton for a few seconds and nodded. His face also showed a sign of relief.

Lan turned around and smiled again at Fenton. The general's face turned serious. Every time, Lan smiled it meant trouble, Fenton knew.

Lan pulled a small note from his briefcase. "During one of our drug smuggling operations, I could not go with Captain Fenton to collect my share of the payment from the Corsicans."

Lan held the paper in the air so that Fenton could see it. "Captain Fenton told me not to worry and gave me what he called his personal note for ten thousand

American dollars. I still hold the note since he never paid me that particular share."

Fenton looked sick. He could not believe that note would come back to haunt him.

Senator Pike looked shocked at the note still held by Lan. "Just what was your share of these drug transactions, Mister Lan?"

"Ten percent of every transaction."

"And how long were these smuggling deals going on?"

"Eighteen months," Lan said.

Senator Pike made a note. "What did you do with all your money?"

"Senator, I never considered it my money. I used it to buy weapons and ammunition for my battalions."

Lan walked to the Senator and handed him the small handwritten note.

Senator Pike read the note aloud. "I promise to pay the sum of ten thousand American dollars to Binh Lan." The Senator shook his head slowly. "It's signed Captain Miles Fenton and dated February 3, 1968."

Senator Pike and the other Senators looked with disgust at General Fenton.

"If we pay your expenses, can you come to our country again to testify in a trial?" Senator Pike asked.

Lan turned around to face Fenton. "If it is General Fenton's trial, it will be my pleasure."

"All records from these proceedings will be turned over to the Department of Justice for investigation of General Fenton," Senator Pike said

"I object," Fenton's attorney shouted.

Senator Pike rapped his gavel. "This hearing is adjourned."

Fenton looked pale. He and his attorney argued as they left the premises.

Bellman, the WestSky executive, slowly walked up to Frank and offered his hand. "Please accept my apologies. As soon as I get back to my office, I'm recommending you be returned to full flying status."

Frank slowly shook the executive's hand but remained silent, remembering the cold shoulder WestSky's executive officers had given him throughout his ordeal.

Lan walked over to Nicole and Frank. "Please understand, Mister Braden. I did not come all this way to help you. I came only to pay my debt to the general. Again, I must apologize for your brother's death. He was a victim of the misfortunes of war."

Frank nodded grimly. "I'm glad I wasn't on your list. You carried out those other executions quite proficiently. I assume you're not going to try to physically eliminate Fenton?"

"Never assume anything, Mister Braden," Lan said. "But dishonoring the General in front of his own people, I feel is more punishment than death."

Nicole gave Frank a slight nudge.

"I want to you meet my wife, Nicole."

Lan bowed and grasped Nicole's extended hand in both of his. "I am honored to meet you. Your husband is a very brave man."

When are you scheduled to return to Vietnam?" Frank asked.

"My plane leaves Saturday afternoon. I do not look forward to it. It is a long twenty- hour flight."

"We're not scheduled to leave until tomorrow," Frank said. "Will you join us for dinner tonight?"

"It will be my pleasure," Lan replied graciously.

"Good. We'll meet you in your hotel lobby at seven."

25

With their victory over Fenton, Frank and Nicole glowed with victorious exuberance in their hotel room while dressing for dinner that night. Frank now regarded Nicole in an entirely different light than he did several weeks previously. He knew that if it hadn't been for her support and love either he would have been dead or under indictment for trying to sabotage an airliner. He watched her dressing from the corner of his eyes, wondering how he could have ever thought of leaving her for something younger. She was just a downright sexy, clever lady.

Nicole, aware of the glances from Frank, walked over to him, nibbled teasingly on his ear and whispered; "I bet you could get us a free hop to Hawaii for this weekend."

He grinned and hugged her tightly.

Nicole placed Frank's face between her hands. "Somehow we won. It's over. You have completely avenged your brother, right?" She quickly kissed him as he tried to nod his agreement.

"But I'll feel better when they send Fenton off to Leavenworth to rot," Frank said.

26

Lan, fit and trim, appeared to be ten years younger than his 75 years. In his dark suit, white shirt and tie, he could easily pass for a senior partner in one of today's successful technology firms.

Nicole, looking elegant in a red strapless dress, knew that she had captured the admiration of Lan that evening during their light dinner conversations. As they waited for their after dinner coffee, Nicole ventured to elicit more facts about the past from this interesting guest. "I heard a little about a girl named Suzi who worked for you and was in love with one of my husband's pilot friends. Could you tell me about her?"

At that time the waiter came with coffee and tea. Lan waited until the server had left before he spoke in a moving, almost inaudible voice. "Her name was Nguyen Kim Mai. Her mother fought in the same Vietminh battalion with me against the French before she was killed. She left a daughter that I raised. Your husband knew her as Suzi, her stage name. I looked upon her as the baby daughter I lost in that French-Indo China war."

"I understand that Suzi was murdered," Nicole said softly.

"Yes, by the Pathet-Lao for revealing secret plans to your husband."

"Oh, my god," exclaimed Nicole. "How did the Pathet Lao find out that she talked to Frank?"

Lan looked at Frank and replied calmly, "Your husband told them."

Nicole appeared stunned. Both she and Lan turned to Frank for an explanation.

Frank looked puzzled. "How can you say that?"

"I will tell you when you tell me how she came to trust you with such information," Lan shot back.

Nicole could feel the tension rising between the two men as they stared at each other.

Several moments passed before Lan broke the silence. "Please, Mister Braden, I have been most puzzled over the decades why she betrayed her own cause to confide such information to you."

"I think you know some of that answer," Frank said, "since you permitted her to fall in love with Tom Parker."

Lan sighed. "I thought that would be an advantage to our cause. But where did you fit in?"

"Believe me, it came as a surprise to me too," Frank said. "You see, after leaving your nightclub on my first visit to Vientiane, Tom took me on a drinking tour of practically every honky tonk in the city. I could barely crawl into my bed that night in my hotel room when we got back. I think he did that on purpose. The next morning Tom took off on a flight on what I believe was a poppy run while I was zonked out in the hotel."

"I think he was trying to keep you alive," Lan said in retrospect.

"Perhaps, but I was astonished at what happened that morning in my hotel room."

Late that morning, I opened eyes my slowly and looked around at the bare walls of the square hotel room. A three-drawer bureau, its dark brown paint peeling off in flecks to reveal a yellowish teakwood finish, sat against one side of the room. Overhead, I thought the ceiling fan was rotating but I wasn't sure since my head was spinning in the opposite direction. I sat up, causing a dull ache in my head.

I had only a few beers the previous night and I began to wonder if somebody had slipped a knockout drop into my drink. Parker had taken me to several bars on the strip. I willingly went to every one except the last one. Even in my wobbly condition, I refused to enter. I remembered that was the one with the French sounding name that was operated by a certain Madame who specialized in oral sex. Air America pilots had warned me about the Madame's bar earlier that evening.

I climbed slowly out of bed and gingerly walked to the window. My mouth felt drier than dust. A knock on the door interrupted my thoughts.

Thinking it was Parker, I walked to the door in my jockey shorts, removed the chain and flung it open. In front of me stood Suzi.

I ducked behind the door and leaned my head out around the edge. But Suzi had already entered the room and now stood behind me.

"Good morning," Suzi said as she sat down on the bed, casually crossing her long limbs while she eyed my lean frame. "You have nice legs."

"Uh, thanks. You, too," I said as I struggled to get a bare foot through one of my pant legs. Not an easy task since the room was still spinning.

She took out a cigarette and lit it. "I have a favor to ask."

"Sure."

Suzi reached inside a beach bag and handed me a Polaroid camera. "I need you to take pictures of me to give to Tom."

"As soon as I get my shoes and shirt on we'll take it outside the hotel by those trees. Where is Tom, anyway?"

"He went flying. Captain came in last night on a commercial flight and needed Tom to fly out to a village."

"Captain? What captain?"

"I believe you call him your XO."

Hm'm, I thought. Did they go to pick up a poppy shipment? Then Tom is really involved. Was I given a Mickey Finn so I'd be out of the way today?

I continued to struggle to get my first leg in my pants. "I'll be ready in a jiffy and then we'll head outside."

Suzi wasn't waiting. She removed her blouse and skirt and kicked off her shoes. She now stood before me wearing a low cut brassiere and extremely brief panties.

"I am not shy."

"I won't argue that."

"Mind if I lie on your bed?" Without waiting for an answer, she lay down on her back and gave me a very sexy 'do you want me' smile.

I blushed and stammered. "I don't think this is a very good idea."

"Please take romantic pictures of me on the bed."

"You know, Tom is my friend," I reminded her.

"That is why I want you to take picture of me. What did you think?"

I took a deep breath to collect myself. "I just didn't know what kind of photo you wanted," I replied as I raised the camera and shot several flash photos. As the pictures merged into focus, I knew that Suzi could have been a top professional model.

After the last picture, Suzi dressed and placed the photos in her bag. She then looked seriously into his eyes. "I know now that you are his friend."

A mischievous grin crossed my face. "What if I had tried to get into that bed with you?"

"You would be permanently wearing parts of this camera."

Suzi then sat back down on the bed, staring at the floor as if contemplating what she was about to say. "Now I tell you real reason I came," she said in a lowered voice.

"First, promise me you will only listen. Do not ask questions on what I am about to tell you."

I nodded, sensing that the girl was about to put her life on the line.

"I tried to warn Tom but he just laughs at me. You must help Tom to stay out of any Vietnamese city, especially Saigon, at the start of TET."

When Suzi said TET, I shrugged my shoulders. "What's that?" I had only been in country for less than a month and I wasn't too knowledgeable yet on their holidays or other celebrations.

"Big Vietnamese celebration."

"When?"

"January 31. I have friends on the other side. They are planning big attacks inside Saigon and other cities." Suzi's eyes clouded with moisture as she spoke, but she continued in a soft but firm voice. "Many in the cities will die. You and Tom stay on your base that night and the following day and you will be safer there. That is all I can tell you."

"The VC isn't strong enough to do that. Will they get help?" I demanded.

Suzi put her finger to her lips.

"I cannot tell you any more than what I have heard,"

Suzi lied. She jumped off the bed and headed for the door where she stopped and turned. "Remember, you take care of Tom for me."

"I promise if you answer one question honestly. It's not related to what you just said," I quickly added. "Is Lan involved in smuggling?"

"Lan involved in everything."

"Is Tom?"

"Some pilots in your unit are."

"What about Tom?

She quickly turned and closed the door behind her shutting out further questions. I heard her run down the hallway.

I thought about the warning. I already had heard many rumors of would-be attacks that came from hooch maids, enlisted men's girlfriends and even from young street urchins, all of which never materialized. But Suzi was a very intelligent woman with a strange background. Her warning seemed authentic. I pulled out a calendar card from my wallet. It read January 28.

"Oh my God," Nicole exclaimed still looking at Frank. "You knew about TET before it happened?"

"A lot of good it did," Frank replied.

"If I had known that she had told you this information, you would never have left Vientiane alive and Suzi probably would have been alive today," Lan said in his usual solemn tone.

"But I did and you even flew on the same flights with me from Vientiane to Da Nang to Saigon," Frank countered.

"How ironic. You flew to Saigon to warn your people of the forthcoming attack and I traveled with you to lead the attack on Saigon," Lan said.

"Excuse me," Nicole said, "for finding your accounts fascinating, almost unbelievable. Why didn't Tom believe you or Suzi?"

Frank shrugged his shoulders. "The same reason you used the term, 'almost unbelievable.' I tried to convince him on our flight back to Da Nang but he just thought Suzi was just overreacting to some rumor she heard."

"Did you give the information Suzi gave to someone in charge, so to speak?" Nicole asked.

"Of course. First thing I did was to arrange a flight to Saigon to get it to our intelligence section at Group Headquarters" Frank then looked at Lan. "That's when I found you that you were on that same flight to Saigon."

Lan nodded.

"In fact," Frank said, "I remember asking you why you didn't take a direct flight from Vientiane to Saigon aboard the commercial 'Air Vietnam' jet instead of flying with us from Vientiane to Da Nang and then to Saigon aboard our old and slow Otters. And you gave me a cock and bull story about not wanting to go though customs because of the bribes you would have to pay."

Lan smiled. "It is a partly true story. I would have been required to pay bribes but mainly I was wary of Vietnamese officials finding out who I really was."

Lan's smile disappeared when he related that he had second thoughts about Frank's appearance on that same flight. "I was going to Saigon with vital TET information for my troops and I wondered if this unusual American with CIA ties was attempting to follow me. If so, I planned to kill you once we entered the Cholon district."

"Thank God I didn't enter the Cholon district by accident," Frank joked.

"The Cholon district?" Nicole said. "Isn't that the Chinese district in Saigon?"

"You are correct," Lan said. "More than a million ethic Chinese lived in the squalor of that distinct. The streets were unmarked, and shacks, tents and houses were rammed tightly on top and against each other without addresses. It is very easy to get lost in Cholon and a good place to hide. It is where your GI deserters hid out during the war with their bar girls and drugs."

"What did your intelligence officers say when you told them about TET?" Nicole said.

Frank smirked. "Well, it certainly didn't set off any alarm bells."

"Who did you get to talk to in that headquarters?" Nicole said with a puzzled look.

"Would you believe a lieutenant."

"I bet he got relieved of his duties after TET," Nicole said

"Nope," Frank replied, "and neither did his superiors."

"How come?"

Throughout this segment of the conversation between Frank and Nicole, Lan listened with an ever so slight knowing smile on his lips. Finally, he spoke. "Simply, the Saigon Vietnamese authorities didn't want to believe it because it would destroy their holiday plans."

"I believe that's true from what I found out at Group Headquarters," Frank said. "I did everything I could and I was made to feel like 'Chicken Little' warning about the falling sky."

After landing in Saigon, I immediately went out through the terminal doors and found a taxi waiting outside. I told the driver to take me to the 23rd Aviation Group Headquarters. The tiny Peugeot sputtered off into the night and turned left down Cach Mang Street. Fifteen minutes later I rang the night bell at Group Headquarters. For an extra dollar's worth of piasters, the cab driver had agreed to wait.

After a minute or two, a night duty clerk unlocked the double glass doors. I explained that I had to see the duty officer on a matter of utmost urgency. After checking my ID card the specialist led me past the duty NCO office where a sergeant sat reading a magazine. We proceeded down a long, dimly lit marble hallway and into a darkened office where a man lay asleep on a cot. The enlisted clerk snapped on a bright overhead light, yelling loudly, "Sorry to wake you, sir, but this person said it's urgent." He left the room, grinning.

A chubby first lieutenant rose abruptly to a sitting position. He couldn't have been more than twenty-two. But the combat infantry badge on the left jacket pocket of his neatly pressed jungle fatigues showed that he had been in at least one firefight if not more. The black tips of his jungle boots were shiny enough to reflect the overhead light. He quickly brushed his short blond hair into place when he saw me. He stifled a yawn with his hand and unsteadily rose to his feet.

"Really sorry to wake you, lieutenant," I said, "But I need to see the S2 immediately. I have some urgent information on an impending attack. I'm CW2 Frank Braden from the Otter platoon at Marble Mountain."

"Oh, a warrant. Good. For a minute I was afraid you were a field grade type, disturbed because I got some winks." He walked over to coffee pot sitting on a hotplate. "How about a cup?" When I declined, he poured himself some coffee into a cup and walked over and sat down at a large desk. "Name's Scott. Just came out of the field myself a few weeks ago. Served in the boonies for six months with an infantry outfit. But you're in luck; I'm now the assistant S2 in this la-la palace. What's the information?"

"I just got back from Vientiane and there's a very intelligent French-Vietnamese woman there who warned me that the VC are planning major attacks on cities throughout 'Nam during the start of TET."

I paused to see if the lieutenant was writing any of this down. Although the officer fingered the pages of his night report logbook, he wasn't writing. He had a skeptical look.

"I see. What's her source.'"

"She said she knows people on the other side."

"Uh-huh. Did she identify them —?"

I shook my head. "No."

"What's her name?"

"She goes by the stage name of Suzi San."

"A dancer?"

"Singer."

"Do you believe her?"

"Yes."

"Is she your girlfriend?"

"No."

His face took on a puzzled frown and he leaned forward on the desk. "Why would she tell you this?"

"Her lover is my friend," I explained. "She was upset that he wouldn't believe her and she wanted me to help protect him. Warned us to stay out of the cities. She was very serious."

At this time, the lieutenant started writing in the logbook. A minute later he finished and looked at me. "I'm not going to call the S2 tonight but I will put a notation on his desk to read the logbook on this subject the first thing in the morning. Where can you be reached if he needed to talk to you?"

"Hmm, probably the Brink BOQ."

The lieutenant reached over to a desktop basket and pulled out a paper. He handed it to me. "As you can see, we have received other information about pending TET attacks. Vietnamese military officials have ignored them. They call them enemy scare tactics." He shrugged his shoulders. "The Vietnamese have gone ahead and released half of their troops and police force for the TET holidays. Even our people don't take it seriously."

I looked at the paper. Its contents read that a captured enemy document addressed to subordinate party members of the National Liberation Front Forces exhorted the VC to fight bravely and aggressively in their forthcoming military attacks against towns and cities, especially in Saigon. It mentioned that the attacks would be part of the final phase of the revolutionary war and that they could count on help from the local population. It showed no date or time for the planned attacks.

When I looked up, the lieutenant shook his head slowly. "After being out in the boonies, even though we kicked their butts in every major engagement, I believe they could mount a short offensive."

He picked up a pencil and tapped it on the desk. "But they can't match our firepower. It'd be suicide for them to come out into the open and attack a defensive force without a three-to-one advantage. Plus, they don't have air cover."

I watched as the lieutenant leaned back into the chair with his hands locked behind his head. He seemed pleased to be able to cite infantry textbook tactics to someone.

"Furthermore, if any attacks did come, it wouldn't be at TET," the lieutenant said with conviction. "They need all the support of the populace they can get." Unclasping his hands, he sat up straight and raised a finger to emphasize his next point. "They wouldn't want to tee off the civilians by fighting on the most honored of Oriental holidays."

He stood up, smiled, and offered his hand. "Thanks for your report. Sorry I can't be more encouraging as to what will be done with your info, but I'm not the engineer of this train. I'll get it on record along with all the other stuff we've been hearing about."

I nodded.

So it'll be looked upon as another rumor. Yet, I still felt adamant about the urgency of her warning. I sensed that Suzi knew a lot more than she told.

As the lieutenant led me along the hallway to the door he said, "If it's any comfort to you, I did hear through our grapevine that we're upping our alert status a notch tomorrow and putting on an extra guard or two at key sites." He stopped at the door and shrugged his shoulders again. "Myself, I think they may try an isolated sapper attack or two, but nothing big enough that will allow us to claim that they violated their own TET truce."

I walked out to the waiting taxi and told the driver to go to the Brink BOQ. I leaned against the back of the cab seat, relieved to have passed on Suzi's warning, but at the same time feeling disappointed and acutely uncomfortable that the threats were taken so lightly.

In a few minutes, the taxi stopped in front of the Brink BOQ. It stood seven stories high in an "L" shape design and boasted a rooftop restaurant featuring GI chefs. As the largest BOQ in Saigon, the longer portion of the building faced Lam Son Square and its shorter section that formed the base of the "L," lined up with Hai Ba Trung Street. Not a particularly aesthetic design, it resembled one of those narrow, concrete coastal "tourist" hotels which face the ocean along Florida's Gold Coast. Outside doors to the individual rooms were located on a long balcony running the length of each floor. For the officers living there, it was centrally located, just one to two blocks away from the old Continental Palace Hotel where Graham Greene wrote the 'Quiet American.' The infamous Tu Do Street with its numerous bars and massage parlors were a block west.

"And that's where I spent TET, confined to the BOQ building, while snipers took pot shots at us for three days," Frank concluded.

Nicole sipped her coffee silently, not wanted to break the spell of hearing these experiences.

Lan smiled. "It is a strange destiny that we meet today as noncombatants. I spent TET encouraging my troops to fight even though I knew in my heart that we were doomed to failure from the start. It was in a dingy Cholon room that I urged my VC troop commanders to fight until they were relieved by troops from North

Vietnam. Troops that those on the Central Committee in Hanoi knew would never come."

"You see," Lan continued, "I found out later that their true purpose of the TET offense was not to score a permanent victory but to inflict lots of American casualties at the expense of their VC brethren in the South. We lost 60,000 or more of our soldiers during TET and it destroyed the backbone of our Viet Cong troops. But the six thousand American casualties were too much for the American public and it was the beginning of the end for United States involvement.

"I do not deny that TET was a military miscalculation by Hanoi," Lan said. "But our efforts surprisingly scored a psychological victory over your nation. It showed us that your home front is weak and has no staying power." Lan leaned forward, placing his elbows on the table. "See, it is your own system which betrays you. Your nation is afraid to lose men.

"General Giap told us that we have the manpower resources to bleed the Americans for twenty more years or until America agrees to withdraw on our terms. Loss of life does not bother us. So, TET was, indeed, a victory for us."

Frank nodded toward Lan. "Your side deliberately violated the cease-fire period that they proposed."

Lan smiled. "Did not the West write the rules for treachery in Machiavelli's book, 'The Prince?'"

"I remember instructing our VC commanders as if it was only yesterday when I paced up and down in front of two blackboards deep in the heart of the Cholon district. One board was covered with the city map of Saigon and had a number of red circles on it. Chalk marks listing designated military units were displayed on the other board. Listening intently to my every word were a dozen commanders, some young, some middle-aged. The squatting men either wore a red armband or had their top shirt button fastened for identification."

Lan had a wistful 'what might have been' appearance while he spoke. "For a while even I thought we might take Saigon by surprise." He slapped a fist in his hand. "We had infiltrated 5,000 men inside the city and had twenty-five battalions attacking the perimeters around the city. We had ambush sites set up to keep the 101 Airborne Division at Bien Hoa from coming to the city's aid.

"Our Sapper and infantry battalions simultaneously attacked the National Radio Station, the U.S. Embassy, the Presidential Palace and the Tan Son Nhut Airport.

"Every police station in Saigon was under attack along with the ARVN artillery and armored complex. Once we had taken that complex, we had trained comrades from the North to man the captured tanks and artillery pieces to assist us. Unfortunately, we could not get inside the complex during the battle."

"How frightening," Nicole blurted out before she could restrain herself.

"That is war," Lan reminded her. "It is brutal. And remember, except for fate, I would have killed your husband without qualm had I known the information he carried."

"Like you ordered the Pathet Lao to kill Suzi?" Frank said.

"I could not prevent that."

"And why do you keep insisting that I'm responsible for her death."

"Because you are. And what I am going to tell you is painful for me to remember but here is how it happened."

I paced the tiny bedroom atop my headquarters in the Cholon district. I had been unable to nap that afternoon and had slept little during the past week. Even at this late afternoon hour, a full seven days after the TET offense had failed, I could hear the sounds of automatic weapons fire and explosions coming from yet another sector of the district. I knew instinctively that one of the many ARVN battalions had apparently uncovered another small band of VC holdouts. They might even be some of my people and I couldn't help them.

As I had predicted, TET had been a costly failure. My units had suffered heavy casualties and had little to show for it. Whereas before I had commanded efficient, confident fighting battalions, I now headed a small collection of beaten survivors whose total number equaled no more than half a company. Worse, they knew they had been misled by lies and false promises to fight in the open against overwhelming firepower.

And, despite the heroic efforts of Lan's battalions, members from the central committee were paying him an official visit today. Lan knew that meant a reprimand, an investigation, or worse.

A knock came on the thin wooden door to my room and I heard the voice of my aide, "Colonel, you have two visitors."

I opened the door and proceeded down the steps to my command and control center. My posture became ramrod straight when I entered the room and saw two men wearing almost identical white suits. "Comrades, you wish to see me?"

The shorter and older of the men stepped forward. "Colonel, we will dispense with formalities and get right to the point. You have a counter-revolutionary on your staff."

I showed no emotion. Did they know about Suzi? After Fenton had contacted me by phone, I had planned to secretly reprimand her for allowing her youthful passion to supersede her dedication. The stupid captain had wanted me to beat her to find out if she had told that new pilot anything about their smuggling operation. Fenton never guessed that he had called an enemy combat operations center to find him.

I figured that she had revealed only enough to protect her American lover, not to hinder the offensive. I knew she was no traitor. The surprise attack had occurred as planned. Of course, I knew that had it been anyone other than Suzi, I would have personally executed him or her. And these men standing before me would be the least likely to understand or forgive such a transgression.

"What is your source?" I demanded. "A traitor would have revealed our most important plans. Yet our TET offensive achieved the element of surprise."

The small man stepped nearer and looked directly into my eyes. "It almost didn't. Fortunately, the over-confident Americans did not believe her."

"Her?" I felt hollow inside as my fear for Suzi intensified. How could they know?

"Your singer and confidant, comrade. The woman the Americans know as Suzi, Nguyen Kim Mai."

"Impossible." I declared loudly. "I have known her since she was a child. I knew her mother who was a dedicated member of the party. She is like a daughter to me."

"Exactly," the small man answered back with a sneer. "You are like a father to her and that is why you cannot see her deception."

"I trust her implicitly. On what do you base your accusations, comrade?"

"The American intelligence officer at the 23rd Aviation Group foolishly phoned his counterpart at the Vietnamese intelligence headquarters and inquired whether they had any background on her. He referred to her as giving warnings about a TET offensive."

The small Vietnamese turned and looked at his partner before continuing, "We have the capability to monitor all their calls."

I knew I could protect Suzi no longer. But I could warn her to flee, perhaps to France where she had friends.

"I will deal with her when I return to Vientiane," I said in a low but grave voice.

"She must be made an example of what happens to traitors," said the political commissar. "You understand that?"

I lowered my head and nodded, worrying that both of these somber men were still withholding something.

"Then you agree," the man persisted.

"Yes," I said, trying to keep the annoyance from my voice.

"Good. Consider it done."

"What do you mean?"

"In view of your relationship to her, we have requested assistance from the Pathet Lao in Vientiane to handle matters. It will be best this way."

I suddenly whirled around, turning my back on the agents, and walked to my desk chair and held onto its back for support. I didn't want them to see the shock in my face. "How dare you suggest I cannot be trusted," I said.

"We also decided that you must remain here for another week—."

"A week," I almost panicked. "I must get back to —."

"A week, comrade," the man persisted.

I sat down heavily in the chair and stared at the wall. For the first time since the death of my own wife and child, a solitary tear weaved down the tiny creases lining my face. My only hope now was to reach her by phone. I turned and faced her accusers.

"If you insist." I got out of the chair and walked the men to the door.

"There is one more thing, colonel. As this happened in your command you will be under house arrest until the punishment phase of the girl is carried out," the small man said. "Not that we think that you would try to warn the girl." He opened the door and waved three men inside the house. "One of these men will be with you at all times until further notice, colonel."

"It was the most tragic day in my life," Lan concluded.

Frank looked apologetic. "I had no idea that your side had bugged the phones of our Vietnamese intelligence counterparts. Of course, I didn't know that our conversation about Suzi would leave our intelligence group. You know I tried to rescue her shortly before her death."

"That is something I am not aware of," Lan said, somewhat surprised. "Please tell me about that. It might ease the pain of my memories."

27

I had been scheduled to fly a solo flight to Vientiane to pick up and return an Otter in which the vacuum system failed. Of course, I didn't know nor did Tom know that the mission was a set up to give me a sabotaged plane on my return flight in which I would disappear over the mountains. According to the aircraft's crewchief, Butterworth, the plane's radios also were inoperative. Prior to take-off from our airfield at Marble Mountain to Laos, Tom gave me a note to give to Suzi and Sergeant Wilson handed me a small light package for Butterworth.

Ironically, I asked Wilson if the package contained marshmallows since it was so light. Little did I know that the package actually did contain marshmallows so that Butterworth could drop them into one of my three fuel tanks to gum up the carburetor in the engine. They knew exactly what fuel tank I would be using over the mountains.

But I gladly took the flight since it gave me a chance to talk to Suzi again. But when I walked into the dim interior of Lannie's and sat down at one of the empty tables, a young woman who had been sweeping behind the bar came over to me and said, "Me sorry, but we do not open yet."

"That's ok, I'm just here to see Suzi."

The girl stepped back and stared at me suspiciously.

"Suzi no here today."

"Is she sick?"

"Suzi no see anybody today. You go."

"Tell her I have a letter from Tom." I pulled out the letter and held it up.

"You friend of Tom?"

"Yes."

The woman left and disappeared through a door near the stage area. A few minutes later Suzi came over and sat down at my table. Without makeup Suzi's face looked pale. Puffiness under her eyes made it appear as though she hadn't slept in days.

"Where is Tom?" She asked me in a voice barely audible. "I need him bad. Why he not come with you?"

I shook my head and explained how this flight came up unexpectedly and that he couldn't get away from his flight instructing duties. "Suzi. You don't look good. What's wrong? Have you been sick?"

"Remember I told you about TET," she said, looking carefully around at the empty ballroom. "Somehow, the people behind it found out that I talked about it."

"Then you're in danger."

"Friends have warned me to leave Vientiane. They said people from the Pathet Lao have been asking about me. I am afraid."

"Then you best leave, quickly."

"Not without Tom," she replied.

"But you can't stay here. They'll find you."

"I know."

"Then you have to leave."

"Not without Tom."

"Damn it. They'll kill you," I warned. "Look, I'm taking

a plane back tomorrow and you're going to be on it."

"Can you do that?" She replied her lips breaking apart into what I thought was a long overdue smile.

"Hell, everybody else has. We'll worry about that later. At least, I can bring you to Tom." I had second thoughts on that naturally. Offering to take an undocumented person across international borders is a major offense. Army officials would throw away my jail key once I'm confined.

"I knew you were a good person, Frank."

"I don't know what Tom is going to do with you back in Da Nang but I think I can get our intelligence people to protect you if you want to talk to them."

I noticed that Suzi's body suddenly stiffened. "No, Frank, I cannot betray my own people."

"Even if they're going to kill you."

"Even if they kill me."

I held her by the shoulders. "We're leaving for Da Nang tomorrow. And tonight you'll stay with me at my hotel. And don't worry about me getting amorous, Tom's my friend."

She shook her head. "No, it would not be wise. If Pathet Lao saw me leave with you, they would know that I am getting ready to flee. They would take swift action. You would be in danger. It is better if I met you at your plane tomorrow."

I could only surmise that she might be right. But I tried one more time. "To hell with those idiots, stay with me tonight and I'll protect you."

"No. My way is best."

I could sense that she wasn't going to give in. "Okay, I'll see you at 12 noon tomorrow at the plane."

Frank looked down at the tablecloth, wiped some moisture away from his eyes and looked at Lan. "Hindsight is great, isn't it? If I had only known what was about to happen, I would have forced her to come with me that day. I really liked that woman. She did what she thought was right and to hell with political beliefs or party lines."

Nicole was touched by the compassion she saw at that moment in Frank.

"You would have only killed her if she had managed to make that flight with you since the aircraft was sabotaged. Either way, death was her only fate," Lan said in his quiet philosophical manner.

"That's right," Frank realized. "If she hadn't been murdered, Tom would not have delayed his return flight to arrange for her body to be returned to her home. Instead, he did delay and gave me his flight while he flew the sabotaged plane that was meant for me."

"But what makes me mad was the manner in which she died. Worse, the Lao police made no attempt to apprehend the murderers." Frank said.

"Maybe they didn't have the expertise to know who they were," Nicole interjected.

"They knew and I knew," Frank said bitterly.

It was twelve thirty when I really began to worry. I figured I'd give her until one o'clock before I went into town to look for her. But five minutes later, I gave up and hailed a cab in front of the terminal building.

I knew something had happened to Suzi when my cab pulled up besides Lannie's and I could see a pair of Laotian police vehicles parked outside and a small group of curious people in front.

I rushed inside and pushed away the hand of a Laotian policeman who tried to stop me. I crossed the ballroom and entered the door by the stage. Inside the small bedroom were a uniformed policeman and two men in civilian clothes. They were standing close together over a prone figure lying on a bloody floor.

The men silently parted when they saw me. There lay Suzi. Her nude body bore numerous bruises. A large pool of stagnant blood stained an area underneath her slender throat. A lamp, table and two wood chairs were overturned and lay in broken shambles. Three Laotian letters were crudely printed with blotches of blood on one of the walls near the bed.

The two detectives, one in his fifties and the other about thirty-five, observed me for nearly a minute before the younger man spoke in English.

"Was Nguyen Kim Mai your girlfriend?" He had a notebook and was prepared to write while the older man watched.

I shook my head slowly. "If you mean Suzi, no. I'm a friend of her boyfriend."

"Who would that be, please."

"Tom Parker. P-A-R-K-E-R. He's in Da Nang."

The detective wrote the name in his notebook and looked at his middle-aged partner who pointed a finger at the open palm of his other hand and nodded toward me.

"We would like to see your identification, please."

I reached into my wallet and brought out my military ID card and handed it to him.

The inspector held up the card for the other man to see, copied the name in his notebook and gave it back to me.

I asked if Nguyen Kim Mai was a real name since I only knew her as Suzi San.

The detective repeated my question in Laotian to the older man who again nodded and took Suzi's passport out of his pocket and held it up. The younger man spoke in English again. "That was the name on her passport. Did you know that she was a suspected VC agent?"

I shook my head no. "Who did this?"

"It looks like a political murder because of the lettering on—."

I stared at Suzi's blood on the wall. "What do those letters mean?"

"In Laotian it means NLF. We believe it refers to the National Liberation Front in Vietnam."

"Bastards"

"She was beaten severely before she died." The Laotian paused for a few moments. "And she also was raped repeatedly so several men must have been—." He stopped to listen to a comment from the older detective.

"My superior asked if you knew of any political trouble she might have been in?"

"Yes. She did say that members of the Pathet Lao had been around asking questions about her."

The detective turned around and repeated my answer in Laotian. The translation startled the older man who gave a brisk reply. His assistant nodded and closed his notebook. "That is all we need. Thank you very much."

I couldn't believe it. It looked like the investigation of Suzi's murder was being terminated. "Aren't you going to question people at the Pathet Lao Embassy?"

The younger man smiled. "It is too political for us. You see, she appears to have been a Vietnamese agent. She has nothing to do with our country."

While I looked at him with disbelief, he carefully considered his next words. "As you know, we allow the Pathet Lao to have an embassy here even though we are technically at war with them. In return, they agree not to interfere with the administrative activities of our government here. We do not wish to upset this agreement."

He then emphasized it was impossible for them to take the investigation any further by spreading his hands apart, palms up.

By that time I was visibly shaking with rage. I wheeled around and left the room and returned to the airport.

Frank look at both Nicole and Lan while he continued his story. "When I arrived back at the terminal I wondered how I was going to break the news of Suzi's death to Tom. Inside the terminal, I looked around for a public pay phone. I hated to do it by telephone but it seemed the only way. As I walked across the ramp to tell my crewchief that we would probably be staying overnight, an Otter taxied up and squeezed smartly into a tight parking spot between the other two Otters. Tom stepped out and flashed me his big smile, saying, 'Hey, roomie, I thought you'd be on your way back by now.'

"When I broke the news to him he didn't reply and his face went pale. He sank to the ramp on his knees and lowered his head into hands and sobbed heavily. He really loved her and I guess he had plans to bring her back to the States. I could only kneel down beside him and awkwardly put my arm around his back.

"A few minutes later, he rose to his feet, clenched both fists and raised his arms to the sky. 'Those bastards,' he yelled at the top of his voice. 'And the biggest one of them all is Lan.' He actually spat out that word out. 'They couldn't have done this without his okay.'

"All I could do at that moment was just stand back and think about how I could keep my friend out of trouble and alive, even though he was one of the smugglers. I knew in my heart he couldn't have been involved in my brother's murder. He then told me to fly his plane back and would fly my aircraft back in a day or two. I pleaded to him to let me stay and help him.

"He replied rather coldly that it was his battle and he knew exactly how to handle it.

"That was the last time I saw him. What we did piece together later was that he went to one of the involved Corsican bar owners and borrowed a thousand dollars. He then went to a dive known to cater to Laotian criminals and hired several of them to assassinate you," Frank said, looking at Lan.

"Afterwards he bought a casket for Suzi and placed it aboard my sabotaged Otter and the next day took off to deliver her body to relatives in Dalat. He didn't file a flight plane since he was illegally diverting to Dalat enroute to Da Nang. We figured out that his engine quit somewhere over the Annam Cordillera mountain range bordering Laos and Vietnam." Frank shrugged his shoulders and took a sip of coffee.

"I can fill in part of the assassins' story," Lan said. "The criminals he sent were stupid. There were four of them who followed me to my café after I arrived aboard a commercial flight in Vientiane."

Lan sat back in chair as he remembered the encounter. "I simply went into my office, locked the door, pulled down a door in the ceiling and took the ladder up to the attic which led me to a passageway over the top of the ballroom. I came out behind them on the second floor armed with an AK-47. I watched them go to my office and kick in the door and rush in. I purposely left the ceiling door string dangling so that they would find it. That was to their distress since I had rigged a grenade to the door springs that would explode when the door was pulled down. After I heard the explosion, I rushed into my office and finished off the stragglers."

Nicole's eyes were wide. "Didn't the police do anything to you?"

Lan smiled. "No, I simply went over to the North Vietnamese Embassy and stayed for a few days until the police figured out that the dead men were robbers. They didn't even know I was there since my employees told them I was still in Saigon.

"While I was at the embassy, they told me that they had received a message from one of our jungle battalions near Nha Trang that a barracks maid had warned that Fenton, Wilson and Clyde were planning to get rid of me at the end of their tour."

"So that's when you decided to kill them?" Frank said.

"Yes. I had no idea that it was Parker who hired the assassins to kill me. But it really did not matter since they planned to betray me later anyway."

"And how did you arrange those deaths."

"Prearranged, might be a better term," Lan smiled. "I had already arranged that explosives be placed under the fuel storage tank next the barracks where Fenton

---

and his counterparts always met in case I would need to get rid of them."

" What about the Bobbsey twins and Butterworth?"

"Quite simple," Lan replied. "Your oversexed Bobbsey twins met a couple of new Laotian girls at one of the bars they frequented. The next day they were lured to a secluded area by the girls on the pretext of having a picnic. The women were members of the Pathet Lao Army and the Bobbsey twins were ambushed. Butterworth was easy. He had a male Laotian lover who also was a planted Pathet Lao. The crewchief had his throat cut at night in bed."

"The only two members of the smuggling ring we did not dispose of were Parker who disappeared in the sabotaged aircraft and Captain Wenzel who you dispatched for us."

For a while no one spoke.

Nicole shuddered. "Horrible."

"I am afraid that is the penalty for betrayal in Southeast Asia," Lan said, interrupting the silence that followed the narrative. "Life is cheap over there."

Frank just shook his head. "What they did to Suzi is inexcusable. And that's exactly why I hate any form of a totalitarianism type of a non-elected government like Communism which doesn't have to answer for its actions."

"Do you think that the old monarchy type of government in that aspect was any better?" Lan questioned. "As much as it pains me to hear how Suzi died, the reason why Pathet Lao did it in that fashion was meant more as a warning and to frighten others rather than to make Suzi suffer more."

"I guess that makes it okay then," Frank snapped, glaring at Lan.

Lan, who looked insulted, stood up and bowed politely to Nicole. "I think it is time to prepare for my departure." He turned to Frank, and ever the diplomat, thanked him for the dinner. "Please excuse me." He walked out of the dining room and never looked back.

Nicole watched him leave. "I believe he's hurting considerably more about Suzi's death and the way she died than he ever let on to us."

"Think you're right. He's too loyal to his system of government to let us know how he really feels. It must be hell to keep injustices locked up inside of you," Frank said.

"Hey, enough of this bleakness," Nicole said, leaning over to Frank. "We should be celebrating. We're rid of General Fenton and his henchmen forever. Let's catch a flight home and go pack for Hawaii to celebrate."

28

That evening, Lan, trying to keep his mind off of the newly learned details of Suzi's death, walked down the endless steps of the Lincoln Memorial. He was scheduled to fly back to Southeast Asia the next day and he had been told by his superiors that he shouldn't missed the statue of this American icon at night. After carefully scrutinizing the lighted monument he agreed with their observation. One thing Americans knew how to do is to honor their outstanding leaders, he thought. It almost puts our best memorial to Ho Chi Min to shame.

As he reached the sidewalk and moved into the shadows away from the formidable gaze of Lincoln, a man carrying a 'Please help, I'm homeless,' cardboard sign walked unsteadily towards Lan. He wore clothes that had seen better days.

"Say, I sure could use a dollar, buddy." The transient slurred his words leaving little doubt as to the cause of his homelessness.

But Lan's suspicious nature warned him that something was not right. Why, he did not know until the transient got closer. The man looked too strong and healthy and didn't smell of alcohol. He also wore gloves and it wasn't cold. At his age, Lan knew that he was too slow to run or too frail to fight and he glanced around to see if anybody else was in the area. Seeing no one, Lan shrugged and pulled out a dollar, and replaced the wallet in his side pocket where it was handy. He held out the dollar to the transient and then realized that he had seen the man before.

The stranger smiled when he saw the bill. "Thanks, but I need more."

Lan pulled out his wallet and gave the man a few more dollars. Lan knew he was in serious danger.

"Much more," the man said softly.

"Do you want my entire purse?"

"Oh, more than that."

"It is as I have guessed, then," Lan said sadly. "A dead man wants to kill me."

The man suddenly dropped his slur and answered calmly, "Just as you took the lives of my smuggling buddies." He then withdrew a pistol with an attached silencer.

Lan stiffened and looked his assailant in the eye. "That's over."

"Revenge isn't."

"So, the General sent you," Lan said.

"That shouldn't be a surprise."

"Killing me will not do him any good. Braden is also a witness against the crimes of General Fenton."

"But you're the only witness to murder."

Lan did not flinch as the man fired the pistol into his head. The man looked around, stooped down, and took the wallet from Lan's lifeless hand. He took out all the American dollar bills and threw the wallet down on the ground. He then walked quickly away, leaving another body to support the statistics that Washington D.C. was a crime capitol of North America.

29

On Sunday evening, Frank and Nicole carried luggage, shopping bags, mail and newspapers through the front door of their Austin residence. They left the baggage in the hallway and, throwing the mail and papers on the coffee table, plopped down on the sofa, enjoying the comfort of being in their own home again. Off in the study, the familiar, occasional beep of the phone message machine could be heard.

Nicole turned and looked admiringly at her husband. "What a wonderful three days."

Frank agreed. "Kauai was perfect and you could've given that little woman sex expert, what's-her-name—Doctor or whatever—some magnificent pointers." His smile widened when he saw Nicole blush at the last remark. "Best of all, we were isolated in our own world, no reporters, FBI or stalkers."

The relentless beeping of the tape machine continued.

Frank sighed and got up. "I guess our isolation is over." He walked over to the machine and pushed a button, causing it to report, 'You have ten messages.'

Frank sat down at the desk and picked up pad and pencil. "Frank, call the training section to schedule simulator time so we can get you back on the flight schedule," the voice said.

Frank made a notation on the pad.

The next voice sounded a little more urgent. "Frank, Coffey here. Call my office immediately. This is my third call to you. Where in the hell are you?"

Nicole hearing the message walked into the room and looked at Frank. "What could be so urgent?"

Frank shrugged. "I don't have his home number. I'll leave a message at his office saying we're back."

The other messages, except those from Coffey and a short message from a local reporter, were the usual, from friends and relatives. It was the one from the reporter that got their attention, however.

The short message sent a chill through them. "We got a wire story from AP citing that a Vietnamese official, who testified at a hearing you attended, was found murdered near the Lincoln Memorial. We'd like to get a comment. Please call Bob at the national news desk."

Frank hurriedly went to the newspapers they had brought in and searched through them until he saw the wire story. He silently read the report and put down the paper with a grim face. "Washington police thinks it was a botched robbery. But it seems too much of a coincidence since he was the sole eyewitness to Jack's murder," Frank said bitterly.

Nicole went immediately to the hallway and locked the front door. "It's starting again, isn't it?"

30

FBI agent Coffey phoned the next morning.

"I take it by this time you've heard? Coffey paused.

"Yes," Frank answered. "What effect will it have?"

"For starters, it means that Fenton will walk. His attorney petitioned Federal Court this morning, requesting that all charges be dropped due to lack of evidence."

"Dropped?" Frank nearly shouted into the phone. "The guy's an outright murderer, a greedy drug smuggler and drug dealer. He killed my brother and he probably had Lan killed."

"That's our hunch, too. But the General was conveniently having dinner with an assistant Secretary of Defense at the time Lan was murdered."

Nicole walked into the study and leaned against the wall, listening. Her face was pale, small telltale bags under her eyes indicated a restless night. Her hand holding the coffee cup was shaking.

"The Judge will have no option but to grant the dismissal," Coffey said disgustedly. "Lan was the only eye witness who was still alive to your brother's murder. Under Article 43 of the Uniform Code of Military Justice, his other crimes are void under the five-year statue of limitations. I'm sorry."

Frank brought the phone receiver down to his chest,

stunned. Nicole could see the shocked look in his eyes. Slowly, he brought the receiver back to his ear. "He's getting off Scot-free."

"Not exactly," Coffey replied. "The President's nomination has been retracted and he's being forced into retirement. He's shamed and dishonored by his fellow military contemporaries. You did your country and your brother's memory a great service by exposing him."

"That's not enough."

"I understand," Coffey sympathized. "The whole situation turns my stomach, too. But at least you won't have to watch your back any longer. He has nothing to gain now by harming you or members of your family."

"Except for revenge," Frank said "He showed me that side of him that night when he threatened to get me or Nicole sometime in the future if I testify. You should've seen the look in his eyes when I knocked him down. He's not the type to issue idle threats. I'm responsible for ruining his old smuggling operation and, now, his nomination to a very lucrative position."

There was a pause on the Coffey's end. Finally, he spoke. "I can arrange to get you limited protection. The only other alternative is to get you into our witness protection program. That's rather severe with name changes and disassociation from family members and friends and such."

"No, limited protection wouldn't do any good. He'd just bide his time until the protection was lifted. And, of course, going into the witness protection program would be like suffering purgatory when we didn't do anything to deserve it."

"So, what are you going to do?"

"Defend myself."

31

The retirement party was a sham at the Fort McNair Officer's Club that night. There was no roomful of hundreds of friends and supporters. No speeches, no presents, no award plaques and no time to send out invitations. No afternoon retirement parade with hundreds of troops marching past a reviewing stand with an Army band playing Sousa music. A Department of Army official had simply made a phone call telling Fenton's confused, young wife that the general's retirement was scheduled for the following day and that all paperwork was being processed as they spoke. And that she should tell the general. He'll understand, the official had said.

The general himself was out on the military golf course. When he showed up at the clubhouse, two of the colonels scheduled in his foursome failed to appear and left no message for their absence. This was a no-no in military protocol and full-bull colonels, who hoped one day to make general, would never, under ordinary circumstances, commit a faux-paux like that. But Fenton knew why. Word got around fast in Washington, especially among the upper echelon field grade officers. So, Fenton, the latest Washington pariah, had his aide-de-camp, a major, round up two lieutenants to complete their foursome. The lieutenants, unaware of their host's disgrace, felt honored to have been invited to a round of golf with a four-star.

So the farewell party that night was limited to his aid-de-camp and two other majors who served in his Pentagon office and their spouses along with Fenton and his wife. The partygoers toasted the general while nearby diners at the club wondered what was going on at the general's table. They had not heard the rumors and still had assumed the general was going to be the new Chairman of the Joint Chiefs of Staff. "It sound like the general's retiring," a puzzled officer whispered to his wife at an adjacent table.

Fenton underwent the embarrassing retirement party for Sarah, his wife. She got the group together at the last minute. Sarah, in her late twenties, didn't understand why the Army didn't give her husband a grand sendoff. Married to Fenton for only a few years, she had made no attempt to integrate herself into or understand military social life because she always felt that the older Colonel wives resented her youth and her power over them. But she knew it was strange that he traded the Chairmanship for a quick retirement. She only partly accepted his explanation the pressures that accompany such a promotion should be handled by a younger and more energetic man. He was simply too burned out, he told her.

He was burned, all right, but the fuel was revenge. Braden had cost him millions, unlimited power, and his life's ambition. Most men would have been satisfied to have gotten away with murder and other crimes. Not Fenton. Whenever he felt the loss of the military's highest command clout, his anger intensified. Braden would get his, he swore. Now the question was to decide to go after Braden or his wife. Which would hurt Frank Braden the most, he thought, dying or watching his wife die a horrible death?

32

On an overcast and rainy morning two days later, Frank departed his home heading for refresher training in Dallas at the airline's simulator building. Before he left, he offered Nicole a small .32-caliber Berreta pistol. She shook her head.

"Look honey, I'm going to apply for permits for both of us to carry concealed weapons under the Texas Concealed Weapons' Act. We'll be legal after training by a state approved instructor," Frank explained.

"But we don't have that permit, yet."

"If a worse case scenario arose," Frank said reassuringly, "it'd be better to be alive and illegal than to be dead and legal. I think a jury would understand that. Remember," Frank said, looking troubled, "he threatened you as well as me if I testified. We'll get the ball rolling on the required training sessions just as soon as I return from Dallas."

"What about Susan and Richard?"

"I'm going to drive over and see them at TCU while I'm in Dallas. I'll alert them to the danger. I'll explain the situation to the campus police so that they can keep an extra eye on their dorms."

He handed her the automatic and she accepted it

without further protest and dropped it into her purse. During the three and a half hour drive to Dallas, Frank kept his eye on the rear view mirror. Visibility was bad due to heavy rain showers. It had been raining heavily for the past two days and puddles were forming on the shoulder of I-35, making driving hazardous. Flash flood warnings for low creek crossings on county roads were being updated nearly every 30 minutes on the radio.

Frank figured that the General himself would come after him to save money since Fenton's income was now officially cut in half and any future illegal gains were out of his reach. *Fenton may have a million or two stowed away but he's greedy and won't spend it now.*

Frank didn't have to go to Dallas for training until next week but he wanted to force the showdown now, far from his home. He knew if Fenton didn't come after him himself, it would make things even more dangerous since Frank would have no inkling of what the would-be killer would look like. Worse, Frank knew he would have to capture a hit man alive in order to connect him to Fenton.

He drove slowly, keeping his eye on the rearview mirror. He really believed that Fenton wanted him dead. *What would I do if I were the general, slightly psycho and seething with revenge?* As he passed Waco, the half-way mark between Austin and Dallas, Frank slowed his car down as an answer flashed through his mind. *I'd probably send a killer after Nicole to get to me.*

Frank suddenly felt his throat go dry. He should have never left Austin, leaving Nicole alone. With his thoughts preoccupied with Nicole's safety, he took the next access road turnoff, crossed over a bridge and headed back south down I-35 at a high rate of speed.

Frank called his son at the university on his cell phone and explained the situation about Fenton. He detected an unbelieving tone in Richard's voice but when Frank told him that his mother was also in danger, Richard got serious and promised him that he would be careful and that he would watch out for his sister.

The second call Frank made was to Agent Coffey in Washington. When Coffey picked up the phone, Frank said, "I had a change of heart. We'll take that limited protection. I want it specifically for Nicole. Is that a problem?"

"As I told you, I can't promise you how long," Coffey replied. "What made you change your mind?"

"Knowing Fenton's mind. Look, Nicole's at the hospital now. I'm about a hundred miles north. Can your folks pick it up from there?"

"We'll get right on it." Coffey paused. "Would it ease your mind if we put a tail on Fenton to see that he stays in the Washington area?"

"God would it ever. Thanks. If you ever had to get hold of me quick use my cell phone number." Frank placed his cell phone in the standby mode and breathed a sigh of relief.

33

Nicole took off her white mask and gown and left the surgery dressing room. She hurried down the hospital corridor. It was lunchtime and except for a limited number of people still on duty, the hallway was devoid of the usual number of medical workers and clerks. Her pager had informed her that one of her patients was having difficulty with his pain medication and she was on her way to the patient's room to write another prescription. Coming towards her was another doctor in a surgery gown and mask. Nicole thought it was strange since most surgeons don't put on their masks prior to entering the surgical dressing room.

He walked rapidly passed her, turned around, and grabbed her from behind. Her scream was cut short by a hand over her mouth as her attacker shoved her into a linen closet.

As Nicole struggled against the man she banged her head backwards into his nose. He moaned and briefly released his grip. She darted for the door, screaming. The man again grabbed Nicole and struck her hard over the head with the gun butt, knocking her unconscious. A passing orderly heard the scream and opened the closet door. The assailant shot the orderly three times in the chest. A silencer attached to the barrel of his pistol made the small .22-caliber gun sound like undistinguishable pings. He stepped aside and let the orderly fall into the closet.

There were two dolly baskets inside the closet. He put Nicole and the body of the orderly into separate baskets and covered them with used linen. He slipped on the jacket of the orderly, opened the door, and wheeled the covered Nicole down the hospital corridor. He calmly nodded to a security guard as he wheeled the dolly out the rear exit.

Outside, he pushed the dolly into a rented white van and drove away.

34

Forty-five minutes later as Frank drove south through Georgetown, his cell phone buzzed.

It was Coffey. He spoke quickly. "I want to warn you that we cannot find Fenton's whereabouts. His wife said he left for Hawaii yesterday for a business conference. But so far we haven't been able to confirm that."

A sickening feeling entered Frank's stomach as his worst fear preyed on his mind. "Can you find out if one of your Austin agents has been sent to protect her, yet?"

"I'll get on that and call you back."

Frank quickly dialed the hospital. "I'd like to speak to Doctor Braden, please. This is her husband and it's urgent."

Moments that seemed like an eternity passed. Frank speeded up to seventy miles an hour as he sped through Round Rock. A voice on the phone informed him that Doctor Braden had apparently left the hospital and that they had been calling for her to see one of her patients.

"I'll tell her that when I see her," Frank said as he disconnected and increased his speed to seventy-five. A sickening feeling came up from the pit of his stomach. Damn it, I should have stayed home. He then phoned his home and got only the answering machine. A minute later his cell phone buzzed again.

"Bad news," Coffey said. "Our agent arrived a few minutes ago at her hospital and couldn't find her. Even the hospital personnel didn't know she had left."

"She's in trouble," Frank said.

"I have to agree," Coffey said solemnly. "One of the cleaning personnel at the hospital discovered the body of an orderly dumped inside a dolly in a linen closet. He had been shot three times. I'm getting some more agents down there in on this. I'll call you when we learn anything."

Frank continued to ignore the speed limits and raced through the wet streets to his house. He quickly drove into the driveway. Her Suburban wasn't parked in the garage. Maybe she's sick. He hurriedly went through the back door. The first floor was empty. He ran, heart pounding, upstairs to their bedroom, yelling, "Nicole!"

The door was closed and he quickly opened it. He saw a note on the bed. Picking it up he read the awkwardly printed words. 'If you want to save your wife, follow these instructions implicitly. Otherwise she pays terribly for your transgressions. Drive immediately to the intersection of Ranch Roads 3238 and 12 and wait. Your wife was good enough to loan us her cell phone. It's on the dresser with a state map. Take them and we'll give you further instructions at the intersection if you're not followed by land or air. Time is of the essence. Don't delay. Nicole dies if you don't come alone or quickly. Your phones are bugged and any attempt to contact authorities will result in Nicole's immediate and painful death. Bring this note with you. We don't like to leave a paper trail. And, oh, by the way, have a nice day."

Frank immediately went downstairs to the study and made a copy of the note and left it on his desk. The note's polished grammar but poorly printed handwriting indicated that someone like Fenton dictated the note to a lesser-educated assailant. He figured that Nicole must have convinced them that he didn't have a cell phone and talked them into leaving hers. Good girl.

Frank used his cell phone to contact Coffey and rapidly explained the situation.

"So, what are you going to do, as if I didn't know?" Coffey asked.

"Question is. What can you do without getting Nicole killed?"

"There are ways to track you but they take time to assemble. We have an old Army plane with its side looking airborne radar that's capable of tracking any traffic in that whole area while it's fifty miles distance. And it transmits vehicle movements to us simultaneously. They'd never see nor hear the plane but we need a day or two to get it here."

"There's no time. They want me to leave immediately," Frank said.

"Give me ten minutes and I'll have a tracking device placed under your vehicle."

"I'll try."

"What do you have for a weapon?"

"A snub-nose .38 revolver."

"Take a second gun and hide it on your body."

"I don't have any."

"The agent currently on his way to your house will give you a Glock pistol. It's a 9 millimeter, fifteen shot semi-automatic."

Nicole's cell phone rang ominously.

"I gotta go. I'll call you on the road."

"Wait for our agent."

Frank didn't comment and turned off his cell phone and answered Nicole's.

"What's your position," said a voice that sounded vaguely familiar, but it wasn't Fenton.

"I'm leaving the house now. I got sick to my stomach and had to puke," Frank lied.

"Bullshit," came the almost recognizable voice. There was a long pause and then the voice spoke again. "Okay, I figured you for a pussy so you get one more chance. Get your ass on the road NOW!"

"I'm leaving." Frank pleaded. He heard a muffled laugh and then a click at the other end. Frank rushed out of the house and got into his car. Shit, I know I heard that voice before.

Frank's hurried departure was suddenly halted by a late model gray sedan that turned into and blocked his driveway.

Frank leaned out his window, "Get out of the way."

A shorthaired man, about 35, wearing a dark blue suit, jumped out of the car and ran through the rain towards Frank. Warily, Frank touched the handle of his snub nose revolver inside his jacket. The man nodded a greeting and stopped at the front end of Frank's auto. Without a word he quickly bent down and attached a magnetic device under Frank's front bumper. He then moved quickly to the side window and handed Frank another pistol, saying only, "It's a Glock. The best. Good luck."

Frank laid the pistol on the right seat and sped off onto the grass and around the agent's car. The agent made no attempt to follow.

35

Asteady rain was falling again, making the winding Ranch Road 3238 slick but Frank didn't reduce his speed. He needed to quickly get to the designated intersection. He knew that another delay might cost Nicole's life. What he planned to do when he got there he had no idea. His mind was racing as fast as his auto but he couldn't think of a thing outside of rushing to Nicole's side.

At a sixty-degree curve, he braked hard and skidded off the road, down an embankment into an isolated metal frame gate denting his grill and fenders. He busted the chain locked gate open. The crash sent some grazing cattle scattering. No time to close the gate he told himself. The rancher will be pissed but he'll have to round up his own animals. He quickly slammed the car into reverse and climbed back on the road and continued. Trees and higher hills loomed up on both sides of the road now. Where in the hell was that damn road 12. If they already had hurt Nicole, he was going in shooting and damn the results. He now was glad that the agent had reached him in time with the Glock pistol. He just might need that extra firepower.

A small road appeared on his left. He slowed down to examine the small county road sign. It read Ranch Road

12. He stopped and parked on the side of the road. The area was isolated and no vehicles could be seen. His grim-lined face glared at Nicole's cell phone.

Thirty minutes later, the misty rain had increased into a downpour and still no word from the kidnappers. Frank experienced that sickening feeling in the pit of his stomach again as he worried about Nicole. He guessed that his adversaries were being careful that he wasn't followed but the waiting was taking its toll on him. He chewed on a stick of gum faster than the rain-drops hitting his car. After having time to calm down, he figured that they probably wouldn't hurt Nicole until after his arrival. So he decided to place the Glock weapon under the front seat, certain he would be frisked. No use giving up both guns, he thought. At least he would know where to go for a weapon should it be necessary.

About five minutes later, Nicole's cell phone rang. Again, a familiar voice told him that a blue pick-up truck would drive pass shortly, and that he was to follow it closely. "Keep close," the voice warned. "If you lose me, your honey dies."

36

Coffey had flown to Austin aboard the agency's Grumman executive jet. He now stood around a round table with a task force of ten other agents in the local FBI Headquarters.

"As far as we ascertain at this point, he's at the intersection of Farm-Ranch Roads 3238 and 12," related Jack Murphy, 38, a tall agent in charge of the Austin office. Murphy, a six-foot-seven slender fellow, placed his stick pointer at a spot on a map laid out on the table as Coffey watched. "This is the location of his vehicle. It's sitting in the middle of nowhere right now."

"What do you mean sitting?"

"His vehicle hasn't moved for the last thirty minutes."

"What else is out in that direction?" Coffey said.

"Lots of isolated ranches, woods, hills, some summer children's camps. It's called the hill country and the hills get larger as you move westward. About eight miles west is a small Travis County Preserve called Hamilton Pool. Beyond it on Route 3238 are the towns of Cypress Mill and Round Mountain. At Round Mountain the road dead ends into U.S. Highway 281. North of that highway is Marble Falls and south is Johnson City and the west continuation of U.S. Highway 290 to Fredericksburg."

"What's down Ranch Road 12?"

"A town called Dripping Springs. About eight miles distance."

"How far away are your vehicles?" Coffey said.

"About fifteen minutes, sir."

Coffey looked up from the table. "This isn't working. Right now we have no idea that he's even in the vehicle, do we?"

The other agents look around uncomfortably and nodded their heads in agreement.

"Under the time restraints and circumstances, sir,' the agent-in-charge protested, "it's the best we can do."

Coffey breathed deeply. "I think it's time we took a chance and send a vehicle, tractor, pickup truck, anything relevant to the area, to drive past and take a look."

"Yes sir." The tall man picked up his hand held radio and relayed instructions to his waiting field agents. He turned and looked at Coffey. "This could alert the kidnappers, sir."

Coffey nodded, "I got to take that chance. God might forgive me if we do alert them, but Frank Braden never would."

37

Frank, growing more impatient, rolled down the window on the driver's side despite the raindrops splattering over him. That's when he heard the mechanical growl of an old pickup truck coming up behind him. Glancing in the rearview mirror, he saw it. A dirty blue pickup truck headed towards his car. Frank's anxiety increased and he started his engine. But the truck didn't drive pass. It stopped alongside.

Through a darkly tinted window he saw a figure behind the wheel. The figure yelled. "Plan B. Get your ass inside the truck." Frank couldn't distinctly make out the man's face but now he recognized the voice.

Frank exited his vehicle with some reluctance, hating to leave the Glock pistol behind. He had his thirty-eight tucked in the small of his back but knew it was only a matter of time before it would be discovered.

He opened the truck door and his suspicions were confirmed that the voice he had been hearing belonged to the supposedly dead Sergeant George Wilson.

Frank knew then that the story given him by Fenton in his backyard about how the general survived the fuel tank explosion at the barracks was completely fabricated. He wondered how much more was fictitious.

Did the CIA agents Al and Chuck really perish in an aircraft accident? Or were they murdered?

Wilson leaned on the wheel, looking toward Frank with an ominous grin. His eyes, set apart by his large and still zigzagging nose, were devoid of expression. They stayed focused just over the top of Frank's head, giving the sergeant the same menacing appearance he had decades earlier in 'Nam. Despite his middle age, the sergeant had kept his big frame in fair shape.

Wilson rested his large hands on the driver's wheel. "Now I'm not moving this truck until you give me your weapon."

"I don't have any."

"Each second we sit here, the closer your honey comes to dying." Wilson glared at Frank. "And it won't be pretty."

Frank hesitated. After several seconds he reached behind his back and brought out the revolver. For a second he pointed it at Wilson and then reluctantly turned the weapon around and handed to him.

Wilson laughed and put the gun in his pocket. "I don't think you're stupid enough to keep another gun from me. But we're going to check, anyway. Now, step outside and take off your shirt and trousers." Wilson pulled a .45-caliber pistol from his belt and pointed it at Frank. "Don't fight me. Wouldn't do you any good since we hold the marbles."

Frank reluctantly did as instructed and shivered in the rain as he stood in jockey shorts. Wilson nodded and told Frank to put his clothing back on.

As they drove west on the county road, Frank looked over at Wilson. "Okay, how did you survive the blast?"

Wilson grinned again. "Simple, I just followed the captain out the door shortly before the fuel tank erupted.

I figured that if he thought momma-san was up to something, he'd probably be right. We knew that Lan was out to get us. Clyde didn't think so and he stayed put and got fried." Wilson shook his head and laughed again. "Just as well, I didn't like him anyways."

"So you hid out until I left and the two CIA agents died?"

"Yeah, that's about it. No witnesses." Wilson paused. "Except for that Commie Lan. We didn't expect that."

"Then it was you that murdered Lan?"

"Now that was one guy who had it coming. You should've seen the look on his face when he recognized me." Wilson laughed again. "I think he wanted to kill me."

"So, how did the agents really die?"

"Like the General told you. In a helicopter accident. Boy, those things are unsafe to fly, especially when I'm around."

"Meaning?"

"When we found out about their flight, I gained access to the airfield that night and dropped a taped grenade into the chopper's fuel tank."

"So how many died in that?"

"Just those two and the three crewmembers," Wilson shrugged. "What do you think I am, a mass murderer?"

"You're certainly working your way up the ladder. How did you know that the grenade wouldn't go off that night before the flight?"

"Through practice. I knew how many times to wrap the tape around the grenade handle. And the length of time it would take for the gasoline in the fuel tank to loosen the adhesive of that amount of tape." Wilson sounded like he was lecturing a class. "Of course, I had pulled the pin. When the tape loosened and the spring in the handle popped, it exploded inside the fuel tank while the chopper was airborne over the jungle."

"Doesn't killing bother you at all?"

"Boy, I bet that was something to see," Wilson continued with a wistful look in his eye. "The official report read the aircraft went down due to enemy action."

38

When Coffey heard the report that Frank's vehicle was empty. He walked over and stared for a few minutes at the map.

He looked up at Murphy. "Tell me about that Hamilton Pool Preserve."

"Yes sir. Gimme a minute." The tall agent left the room and went to another room where a secretary sat in front of a computer. A few minutes later, he returned.

"It's a 232-acre preserve maintained by Travis County," the agent said. "It's part of what is known as the Balcones Canyonlands Preserve. It's sort of a birdwatcher's paradise. At various times of the year, there's more than 137 species of birds visiting the area. There's a collapsed grotto partially covering a deep pool of water that visitors use for swimming. The whole area sits in a small box canyon with cliffs on both sides. There's also a 60 to 70 foot waterfall at the grotto."

"Anything else?"

"Visitors use a sloping rock trail to the pool area. From the parking lot it's about quarter mile to the pool. There's also another trail going west along Hamilton Creek from the pool to the Pedernales River. It's about a mile long. Incidentally, the Pedernales is at flood stage today and it's rampaging. Strong currents and dangerous. The whole area in the canyon has lush vegetation, primarily ferns, live oak and Ashe juniper trees."

"How many visitors go to the park at this time of the year?"

"Today, the park is closed," Murphy said, "because of the flooding and the wetness on the rock steps leading down into the canyon. Too slippery."

"Any guards live there when the park is closed?" Coffey asked.

"No sir. From what we could learn, there's a tall metal gate blocking the gravel road leading to parking at the top of the steps. When they close the park at darkness or during wet weather, the gate is secured with a chain and lock."

Coffey paced the around the table, holding his chin with one hand. "I got a gut feeling that's where they took them." He turned quickly around and pointed at the tall agent. "Get me two agents who know something about birds, preferably a male and female. Can you do that quickly?"

"I'll see, sir." The tall agent started to leave when Coffey called him back.

"And contact the Travis County Parks District and have them fax you a map of trails in that preserve." The agent nodded and left hurriedly.

"We must assume," Coffey told the other agents, "that all bets are off now. I want the other highways in that area covered by two helicopters and all the cars we have available." Coffey shook his head. "I don't think that Fenton wants to spend too much more time on this. He needs to have some left to cover his Hawaii alibi."

Coffey turned and pointed at three agents. "I want you men to check all the corporate or charter aircraft at the smaller airports in Central Texas to see if any are waiting for the General. There's a chance we cannot save that couple but I don't want Fenton to get out of the area sight unseen. Then we can nail his ass on murder charges."

39

Wilson drove the truck along the hilly and curvy two-lane blacktop with only an occasional glance at Frank. They were in the isolated hill country now and traffic was nearly nonexistent at that time of day. A few ranch houses, setting well away from the road, some hidden by the numerous cedar and small live oak trees, occasionally dotted the landscape along with the cattle. An abandoned wood structure with faded boards hanging down from its tar paper roof and a tilting faded sign reading "Pecans" leaned heavily to one side as they drove past.

Frank spotted the nearly hidden turnoff as Wilson slowed the pickup and made a right turn onto a gravel road. A lock and chain secured a large metal gate in front of them. Frank could see that the gate was attached to a high metal fence going in opposite directions as far as he could see. A Hamilton Pool Preserve sign set on the opposite side of the gate. Another smaller sign on the gate itself announced that the park was closed that day due to hazardous trail conditions.

I guess we climb the fence, Frank told himself, wondering how Nicole could've made it over the high gate.

Wilson got out of the truck and motioned for Frank to do the same. He then went to gate and removed the lock that had been already cut with a bolt cutter. After opening the gate they climbed back into the truck and drove through. On the other side, they exited again while Wilson closed the gate and wrapped the useless lock and chain around it.

Wilson drove in silence down a gravel road to the visitor's parking area. He then veered off onto a service road whose single chain barrier had been cut and headed down a steep road for a quarter mile into the canyon.

"Where's Nicole?" Frank demanded as the truck descended to into the box canyon. Wilson only grinned in reply. In the center of the gorge, abundant trees and lush ferns, along with the rain, made forward visibility extremely limited. Steep limestone outcroppings formed fern-canopied cliffs rising nearly seventy feet, which lined both sides of the canyon. In the center of the horseshoe shaped canyon, a waterfall ran over the top of the grotto, dumping water into the deep dark green pool below. Frank noted the only possible escape route other then the ascending trail and service road was another pathway heading west through the shrubbery along a creek.

As they descended deeper into the canyon, Frank noticed shallow caves were hidden behind gigantic boulders. He figured that Nicole was being held in one of those.

Frank wondered how in the hell he was going to stay alive and still be able to rescue Nicole from these two armed and determined kooks.

40

Helen and William, two agents in their mid-twenties, carefully climbed over the six- foot high fence about a quarter mile from the main gate entrance into the Hamilton Park Pool Preserve. Another agent who drove them to the area in a pickup truck stood by watching them. After they had dropped to the other side, he tossed two pairs of binoculars over the fence.

"Straight ahead is the trail leading to the grotto and pool," he instructed as he examined a park map. "We'll be monitoring your body radios just a few minutes from here. Keep out of sight and avoid direct contact unless the situation warrants it. We really don't know at this time if they're even in the park. If they spot you, they won't know if there are other legal entrances into the preserve. The main gate appears to be chained and locked. Remember, bird watchers," he cautioned, "you can just act amazed when you hear that the park is closed."

"Thanks a lot for the assignment," William snapped, as his one boot sunk a good inch into mud. A darker cloud had moved overhead, causing the wind to increase and the rain to come down in heavier sheets with an occasional cloud to ground lighting strike. Helen, tall and gaunt, smiled ruefully as she pulled her pocket book on birds from a backpack. They put the binocular straps around their necks and pulled their rain jacket hoods over their heads and moved off into the underbrush.

"Happy birding," their driver yelled as a clap of thunder drowned out half his words. He ran to the pickup and jumped in. Inside the cab, he spoke into a microphone. "Our birders are inside the park heading towards the grotto. Should reach there in about thirty minutes."

He drove off towards a rendezvous site about a mile away.

In the dense shrubbery, Helen stumbled and slipped into her partner, sending him tumbling down a hill and into a boulder. He cried out in pain as she ran to his aid.

"Oh, Jesus, I'm sorry," she said.

"Son of a bitch," he cursed.

"How bad is it?" Helen said compassionately.

"I can't straighten my arm. It hurts like hell," William moaned. "I think I cracked a bone, damn-it. Why in the hell did I have to draw you as a partner."

Helen's face turned red. Yes, she had done it again. He was the second partner who had gotten injured on the job with her. But she was only partly responsible for the first injury. She gently looked over his arm before she talked into her body mike. "Birder team has a problem. William fell on a rock and it looks like he broke a bone in his elbow."

"Roger," came a reply over the radio. "Return to the fence line and we'll get you out."

"Negative," Helen said. "William will come back and I'll go on."

"Don't think that's a good idea," the voice said. "You'll have no immediate backup."

"I'll be careful not to be seen if they're in the park," Helen said determinedly. "If that couple is here, they'll have no chance if I come out."

A long pause settled over the radio communications. "Okay. You'll be on you own until I can confirm this with headquarters. Be careful and stay in touch."

Helen helped William get up from the boulder and watched as he slowly stumbled back the way they had come. He didn't say goodbye or wish her luck but simply left her standing there. She hoped he would forgive her when his cast came off. In a minute he disappeared over the top of the hill.

She glumly turned around and headed towards what she hoped would be the trail. Another bolt of lightning struck about a mile away, frightening her and causing her to fall over a tree root. She dropped her flashlight and hit hard against yet another boulder, landing on her body radio. She looked for her flashlight but it apparently had rolled down the hill into the darkness.

The rain splattered against the foliage and except for the occasional thunder, the forest itself was dark, foreboding and silent. Helen instinctively touched the handle of her Glock pistol hidden under her jacket and immediately felt more secure. She still hadn't found the trail yet. Bending low, she picked her way slowly through the underbrush. She couldn't find the trail though it paralleled her path about ten yards away.

Unsure of her position she decided on a radio check. "Base. Commo check from Hotel."

The body radio remained silent.

"I repeat. Base, radio check from Hotel," she said halfway pleading.

No reply.

A deafening crack of thunder echoed off the canyon walls and again caused Helen to jerk up with a start, right into the pointed end of a tree branch. It greeted her face, nearly penetrating her left eye and ripping a scratch mark on her cheek. "Sweet Jesus," she said, wiping a trickle of blood from her face with the back of her hand.

She reached under her jacket and shirt and fiddled with the radio connector wires. After she was certain everything was secure, she tried the radio again. No reply came back.

41

At the bottom of the canyon, Wilson stopped the truck and waved his pistol at Frank to get out. Once outside, Wilson walked around to Frank. "Now march ahead in front of me towards that body of water," Wilson commanded.

"Okay, I did everything you wanted. Now, where is Nicole?"

"You'll soon see her."

Frank moved carefully along the slippery trail, crossing a small pedestrian bridge across the rapidly flowing Hamilton Creek. He then turned right towards the grotto. The trail led around to the back of the rocky cove and out of the downpour. As Frank approached a small open spot by the water, Wilson told him to stop.

They both stood silently for several seconds as raindrops ran down their faces.

"This weather reminds me of the monsoons," Wilson said. "It was on a day like this I shot your brother."

Frank's facial muscles tightened. *That son-of-a-bitch is rubbing it in.*

Ignoring Wilson's taunts, Frank asked, "Okay, asshole, where's my wife and your master."

"My master? Aren't we being cute? Sure, he pays

218

me a top salary but I jump for no man." In anger, Wilson slapped the back of Frank's head hard with his big open hand.

Frank shook his head to clear the blow and turned around and laughed at Wilson.

Growing even angrier at Frank's behavior, Wilson doubled up his fist and was about to strike Frank when a voice from the top of the grotto attracted their attention.

"Are we ready down there?" It was Fenton's familiar voice. He shined a battery-powered roadside emergency light down at them.

"Yes, master," Wilson mocked.

As Frank and Wilson looked up through the heavy downpour, they could barely make out the figures of Fenton and a woman. She appeared to be lying on the ground close to the edge of the cliff with her arms tied behind her back. A gag covered a portion of her face and all of her mouth. A hangman's noose circled her neck. A large cinder block was tied around the bottom of her legs.

As they watched, Fenton, standing in the wind and rain, laughed loudly and bent down. He rolled the woman towards the edge. In a second the figure went feet first over the cliff, momentarily illuminated by a flash of lighting.

"Jesus," Frank gasped.

The fall was quick and short, brought to a sudden jerk above the water by the noose around the victim's neck.

"You just don't know what the general's going to do next," Wilson said, shaking his head in honest amazement.

The lifeless figure, its neck bent at an awkward angle, dangled there, motionless.

42

Coffey sat in the command and control room, monitoring all incoming phone and radio calls. He was puzzled that the agents failed to find any chartered aircraft waiting on Fenton.

He sipped his coffee slowly, staring into the cup's black liquid. I know he's in the area. He has to be behind this. Coffey looked up at Murphy who came into the room. "He wouldn't hire contract hit men to do this. He wants to be personally in on the revenge," Coffey said in a low, thoughtful voice.

"We got several men at the Bergstrom Airport. We also got men at the bus terminal and train station, too," the tall agent said firmly. "No way can he leave Austin by commercial means without us knowing it," the tall agent said.

Coffey got up and walked to the chart table. "I think Hamilton Pool is still our best bet. Anything from the park, yet?"

"We temporarily lost communication with our agent there. She might be inside the canyon and that could cause a problem with the radio we're using."

"Our agent?" Didn't you send in two?"

The tall agent shrugged. "Yes sir, but our male agent

220

slipped on a boulder and broke his elbow. She elected to continue on alone."

"Alone? Is she capable?"

"Uh, that's another problem, sir. We were taking her from field duty and planned to put her behind a desk."

"Why?"

"Well, we think she's smart but somewhat uncoordinated. The last agent who worked with her just got released from the hospital. An accident that was sort of her fault."

"Great."

"As you know, we're shorthanded for this project and we had to use her."

"How can we regain commo? If they're in there we got to know fast." Covey impatiently slammed his hand on the chart. "We're running out of time."

"And manpower," the tall agent said, his face set in grim lines, "We don't have anybody else to spare. We're covering everywhere from Fredericksburg to Marble Falls to Austin and everything else in between."

"What about the park guards? Are they certified peace officers? Maybe we can requisition them to open the park and help us to look around?"

"I think they are. Do you want me to send them out to the park? It could alert the bad guys if they're out there."

"We don't have a choice," Coffey said evenly. "Do it."

43

Frank stared unbelievingly at the limp figure hanging from the cliff. Lightning turned the hanging victim sight into a surreal nightmare. It came into focus out of the blackness every few seconds with every flash of nature's strobe lights.

Frank sunk to the ground on his knees, feeling nauseous, unable to look anymore. He could no longer feel the sheets of rain pelting against him. He had failed to save Nicole.

Even Wilson caught himself feeling sorry for the kneeling figure in front of him. Damn, he thought, the general is just full of surprises. He walked up behind Frank and pointed his pistol at the back of Frank's head and looked up at the general. "Okay, sir?" He yelled questioningly.

"Oh no," I'm enjoying myself too much," Fenton shouted down. "Look at him. On his knees, begging for us to end it."

"General, we don't have that much time," Wilson shouted back.

"Then I'll make time." Fenton laughed and began dancing a small jig, pointing down at Frank. Both Wilson and Frank looked up at the general's antics.

Wilson looked worried and said softly to Frank. "I think he's finally flipped,"

Frank slowly regained his composure as he wondered what would happen when Richard and Susan found out about their deaths. He knew Richard would never rest until Fenton was brought to justice. While Wilson followed the antics of his boss on top of the grotto, Frank grabbed a handful of the pebbles from the calcareous sandy ground. Throwing the debris into Wilson's face and jumping into the pool would be foolish. With his deep water phobia he'd be trapped like a scared fish in a washtub. No, he would wait and see what Fenton had in store for him and then make his move.

Fenton yelled down to Frank. "I got a little surprise for you. All five-feet-six of her." He left the edge of the grotto for a moment and came back holding the tied arms of another gagged female. He picked up the emergency light and shone it in her face.

Frank could scarcely believe his eyes. It looked like Nicole. She had a gag around her mouth and appeared to be still wearing her hospital uniform. But then who was dangling from that noose?

44

Helen heard the din of the roaring waterfall and she thought she heard voices, even laughter ahead. She moved from the trail into the underbrush for better cover.

In another few minutes she peeked out through the bushes and stared at a sight right out of a Hollywood grade B horror flick.

As lighting flashes illuminated the landscape, she saw a big man directly ahead of her pointing a gun at a kneeling figure in front of him. A limp figure, swaying on a rope wrapped around its neck, hung down from the top of the grotto. Following the rope up, she saw the figure of another man on top of the cliff dancing around in circles, laughing loudly. A battery-powered light sat on the ground and illuminated him like a stage actor in the spotlight.

Her glance at the bizarre scene told her that she had indeed stumbled upon the people that she was seeking. She apparently was too late to save the woman. She again grabbed the radio strapped to her body, jiggling it and swearing softly when it remained silent.

Helen quickly analyzed her options. She couldn't expect help from her companions anytime soon. She could shoot the man holding the gun at the back of his victim's head but that would give the dancing idiot at the top of the grotto a chance to escape. And she would have to shoot without warning to prevent the gun holder from eliminating the victim. But shooting without warning would put her career in further jeopardy especially if the gun holder was the airline pilot who had somehow gotten the upper hand on one of his kidnappers. Since she sensed that the kneeling man was not in immediate danger of being shot, she decided to watch and wait for a better opportunity.

On the cliff, the former dancing man disappeared momentarily before he brought another woman to the edge. He yelled down but his words were obliterated to Helen by the roar of the waterfall. She did, however, hear him order the two men below to come up to his position on top.

She watched as the gun holder motioned for the victim to stand up and start walking back towards the service road.

Helen, maneuvering through the bush, followed the two men until they started walking up the gravel road as it curved along to the top of the grotto. She stayed at a distance since the top of the grotto had few trees and little shrubbery.

By this time, rain had found its way through her poncho and had drenched her ball cap, Levis, kaki shirt and boots. She shivered as she crouched in the wet bushes and planned her next move.

45

Frank pondered his options as they reached the top of the grotto where Nicole and Fenton waited. He knew that Fenton had gone too far to back down now. They were marked for death and it was up to him to save them.

As they got closer Frank could see that Nicole's eyes were wild with fright. When she saw Frank, she tried to move in his direction but Fenton held her back.

Fenton waited until Frank and Wilson were only a several yards away before he spoke. "Welcome to my last command," he said bitterly, sweeping his arm over the grotto. "Did you like my mannequin trick?"

"Coffey knows you're in the area," Frank warned. "Give it up before you get deeper in the hole you're already in."

"And give up your court martial?"

"Court martial?"

"I warned you. I gave you a chance to back off and told you the penalty if you didn't."

"You're crazy," Frank said, looking around at Wilson to see his expression and his location. Just maybe Wilson might be have second thoughts about doing the bidding of a man obviously out of his mind.

But Wilson just stood there with a blank expression. Great, Frank thought, we're dealing with two fruitcakes.

"And just for your information, the authorities will never prove that I was in this area. I have a charter helicopter waiting for us in a nearby farm field and an alibi waiting for me in Hawaii."

"Okay, just leave Nicole out of this. This is between you and me."

"You think I'm a fool. It's too late for that," Fenton said, shaking his head. "Besides, it'll be a pleasure to see you watch her die because of what you did."

Frank watched in desperation as Fenton began wrapping a cord around Nicole's legs. She tried to kick him but he tightened the grip around her legs. And to the end of the cord he attached a cinder block.

"I'll retract everything I said about you," Frank pleaded loudly above the noise of the waterfall. "I'll tell them I did it out of a personal grudge. I'll make them believe me. You'll get your command back."

"And miss out on this pleasure?" Fenton laughed. "Please, I hate whiners." Fenton stood up. "And now it is the sentence of this court that the executions will take place immediately."

Frank moved towards Fenton but Wilson quickly came up and placed the muzzle of the pistol against the back of his head. "One more step and you're dead."

Fenton put both hands on Nicole's shoulders and moved her towards the edge of the ledge. She turned and looked at Frank with pleading eyes. "Don't worry, my dear, you're already wet," Fenton said.

A bolt of lighting struck a nearby tree in the reservoir and the four of them instinctly ducked their heads, cringing. Helen used this opportunity to emerge from the bush and ran up the road with her gun pointed at

them. She yelled, "Drop your weapons, stand still, FBI."
Wilson, startled, turned and fired at the figure. Helen
dropped to one knee and shot accurately in return. Wilson fell to the ground, clutching his chest.

Fenton, seeing his chance of revenge rapidly evaporating, picked up the heavy cinder block and hurled it over the edge. The falling weight took Nicole off her feet and Fenton rolled her off the cliff, sending her seventy feet into the dark green pool below. Frank dashed towards the ledge and jumped off after Nicole. He was in the air as her feet touched the water. Fenton, still kneeling, fired a barrage of shots in the agent's direction, hitting her twice. The bullets jerked the agent backwards onto the gravel road and she lay still.

46

The pool water was cold and deep and Nicole rapidly sank the entire twenty-seven feet to the rocky bottom. She desperately struggled with the knot binding her hands in the dark water as her body floated above the cinder block. She had used up about thirty seconds of air when she felt the brush of Frank's body near her feet.

Frank tugged on the rope knot around her legs and knew he could not untie it before their air ran out. So he followed the rope to the cinder block. Grasping the block he repeatedly smashed the cinder block against one of the gigantic boulders on the bottom. After nearly a minute, the cinder block cracked and he slipped the rope out through the break.

Struggling against the now painful lack of oxygen, he grabbed Nicole's tied wrists and kicked for the surface. When they felt their lungs were ready to burst, they broke surface, gasping for air so desperately that the sound was loud enough for Fenton to direct his light down to illuminate them in the water. He fired several rounds in their direction and the water around them kicked up small spurts.

Frank swam hard, pulling Nicole along behind him. He knew that the only way that Fenton could get closer for more accurate shots was to jump in and he knew even Fenton wouldn't want to take that risk.

Fenton seeing that they had made shore, ran down the road but stopped by the limp, silent figure of the FBI agent. He lifted his pistol and pumped another shot into her body. He then came upon Wilson, now sitting up and clutching his chest.

"Jesus, I'm hurt bad." Blood came from his mouth as he spoke.

Fenton, shining the light on him, nodded. "You couldn't even make it to the pickup if I helped you." As Wilson lifted his bloody hand to see how bad his chest wound was, Fenton placed his pistol inches away from Wilson's head and pulled the trigger. Can't afford to leave people behind who could swing a deal to testify against me. Fenton then started to jog down the road toward the parking area, confident that he would cut off Frank's and Nicole's escape route through the parking lot to the main gate.

As Frank sat beside Nicole on the shore, he quickly untied her hands. He could spot the location of Fenton by the bouncing light coming down the road bordering the cliff above him. After taking the gag from her mouth, she cried and hugged him tightly. There, in the pouring rain, they kissed like they never kissed before. Then Frank began to untie the more difficult knot binding her legs.

"Frank. He's practically halfway down the hill," Nicole said trembling, uttering her first words that night to Frank.

Working faster, he unwrap the rope around her legs. He threw the rope to one side and then, as an afterthought, decided to take it with them.

Nicole watched, as the bouncing light got closer to their level. "Let's go." She started running toward the stair path leading upwards to the parking lot.

Frank caught up to her and grabbed her. He pointed her down another path heading west along the south side of Hamilton Creek. "He has the angle to cut us off if we try to make it to the parking lot. I think this trail will take us to the highway."

Frank and Nicole ran into the dark abyss, keeping the rushing creek waters on their right side. Using the illumination provided by the occasional lighting flashes, they stumbled over tree roots and rocks on the trail. In those brief moments of light they could see the nearly vertical rock walls raising on both sides of the canyon, preventing their escape in those directions. Behind them in the boxed canyon were the grotto, waterfall and Fenton.

Nicole, stumbling and slipping over the mud and on the wet rocks, questioned Frank on his choice of escape routes. "What if there is a box canyon at the end of this trail?"

"Trust me. All boxed canyons are only boxed in one direction. Besides, this creek has to flow somewhere."

"Where is the trail? I can't see anything," Nicole said as she stumbled over a large rock again.

"We'll catch sight of it again during the next lightning flash," Frank yelled, pushing her forward. "In the meantime, just run where there's a lack of foliage. That's the trail area."

From a higher ground in the distance, Fenton, during lighting flashes saw his prey run down the canyon. He smiled and knew he had them now.

47

Nicole lifted her feet higher as she ran, trying to avoid the roots and rocks. She felt the terrain descending down a small slope. Lightning flashed, revealing a smooth area ahead, minus the protruding roots and rocks. That's strange but a blessing, she thought.

Her next steps brought water up to her knees. "Frank," she screamed, "go back. We're heading into the creek."

"No, keep going, the creek has flooded the lower trail. It's dry just ahead where it's higher."

Nicole gripped Frank's hand tightly as they waded their way forward. Soon she found a slight incline and emerged from the wetness, happier to be back stumbling over the obstacles than in rushing water in the dark.

In another minute, they came upon two massive boulders, each about twenty feet long and eight feet high, leaning against one another, forming a tunnel arch. They stopped under the arch to catch their breath while escaping the constant pounding of the rain. That is, until Frank spotted a bobbing light coming down the trail they just had covered. "He's about two to three minutes behind us."

Again, Nicole and Frank started their slipping, sliding and stumbling on the path before them. Ahead the trail suddenly split and Nicole took a right turn and followed the path. Frank caught up to her and grabbed her. When lightning flashed again across the sky, the illumination revealed she was standing on a visitor overlook on the edge of a twenty-foot drop-off above the flooded Hamilton Creek. "Never turn right," he shouted above the rushing water. They turned back and took the left trail, continuing their escape.

Fenton, shinning his light ahead of him, cursed and stumbled along the trail. He knew he was catching up since he could avoid most of the obstacles that would slow them down. I got to get this over in a hurry when I catch them. He figured he would shoot Nicole first in front of Frank, just to make him suffer a moment longer. The thought made the rain more tolerable to him. He knew the end of the trail was near as he heard the roar of the water increasing.

Up ahead, Frank wondered why the sound of the rushing creek had intensified. Hamilton Creek was flooded but it shouldn't be making a loud sound like that. He put his hand on Nicole's shoulder and told her to stop.

Nicole had noticed the increasing roar of water, too. "What's that noise? It sounds like Niagara Falls, for God's sake. I also swear I hear a faint siren every now and then."

Frank stepped in front of her. "Let me go first."

He then proceeded ahead, dreading what was uppermost in his mind. He walked right smack into a tree limb, striking his forehead. The thick limb had extended head high out over the trail. As he stopped and rubbed his bruise, a bolt of lightning streaked across the sky. Frank froze in his tracks as the electrical bolt illuminated a rampaging Pedernales River directly in front of him.

Their trail, now steeply descending, disappeared into the swift current. That explained the siren. It was warning campers several miles upriver to evacuate the Pedernales Falls Park. He knew that a flooded Pedernales had the reputation of snuffing out more lives than most of the Texas rivers combined. A couple more steps and he would have fallen from a ledge into the frothing, wide cauldron of raging water fifteen feet below. There was a second ledge four feet beneath the one he was standing on but it was only a few inches wide. As he eyed the water during the flashes of the storm he could tell it was visibly rising inch-by-inch towards them. He knew it was only a matter of a few short hours before the water would reach the place they were standing.

Nicole came up behind him. "Where's the highway?" She started to tremble again when she saw the rampaging river in front of them.

He quietly looked at Nicole with more love than he had shown her in the past decade. "We're trapped," he slowly admitted. Bitterly, he realized he had wasted their time together. Now they had none left.

Nicole stared back into his eyes. "Don't give up, he's only human, too. We can beat him," Nicole said with determination.

Nicole's courage sent Frank's mind's racing. Fenton would be on them in less than two minutes. He figured that the only way Nicole had a chance to live was for him to somehow maneuver Fenton near the ledge and then rush him, knocking them both off the precipice into the river. He hoped his dying momentum would be strong enough to carry them both over the ledge before Fenton's bullets found a vital spot. While he pondered the plan, he fondled the ashe juniper limb that bashed him in the forehead. He then changed his strategy.

Frank unwrapped the rope he had been carrying around his shoulder and quickly tied a knot around the end of the protruding tree limb. While Nicole watched, he moved to the tree and placed the rope around its sturdy trunk. He started pulling the rope, bending the tree limb back towards him. God, don't let the limb break, he silently prayed, as he bent the limb further and further back until it was off the trail. He was holding the rope tightly around the trunk now, feeling the pressure from the stretched limb that was eager to swing back into its normal position.

"Come here and hold onto this rope as if your life depended upon it, because it does."

Nicole quickly moved to his side and took hold of the rope and held tightly onto it. "But won't he see us over here?"

"Not if you keep your body on the other side of that tree trunk. I'll be on that ledge in front of him as a distraction."

Nicole looked at him fearfully. "He'll shoot you the moment he sees you."

"I hope not, at least not for a few seconds. Just remember this. When I jump onto that lower ledge, you just let that rope go."

48

The sound of the rushing water drew louder as Fenton neared the end of the trail. He, too, heard the faint wailing of the rising and falling siren but wasn't quite sure what it meant. He slowed down now, swinging his light from side to side, not waiting to miss his prey hiding on either side of the trail.

He saw a figure dart in front of him and flashed the light in that direction. In the light's beam stood Frank on the ledge, facing him. Fenton saw that the river was immediately behind Frank. He also knew that Nicole had to be off to the side of the trail but he didn't want to shine his light there at this moment until he had shot Frank. Fenton raised his pistol and moved a few yards closer. He didn't want to miss this time.

"We're not going to give you the satisfaction of shooting us," Frank said defiantly. "We're taking our chances with the river." Before Fenton could fire, Frank jumped backwards off the ledge. As he disappeared from Fenton's view, his feet barely hit the narrow second ledge. Immediately crouching down, he dug his fingernails into the clay wall of the bank to keep from falling backwards into the swift current.

Fenton ran forward to look over the ledge, suspecting a trick. He knew Frank wouldn't attempt to try that raging current. At that moment, as he looked down and saw Frank crouching on the second ledge, he heard a swishing sound and the strong tree limb struck Fenton a staggering blow to the back of his head. Stunned by the force of the blow, he catapulted headlong into the swift current where his bobbing form quickly disappeared beneath the murky surface.

Frank saw Fenton propelled over him. He wanted to celebrate, but he didn't move. He wouldn't dare unclench his fingernails from the clay wall lest he became the second flood victim tonight. He could only yell a muffled "help" into the clay where his mouth was pressed.

In what seemed an eternity to Frank, he finally heard Nicole's voice. She was kneeling down and peering over the upper ledge. "I don't think I can reach that far."

"Throw the rope over the ledge," came Frank's muffled voice.

When Nicole dropped the rope it dangled over his back. Taking a deep breath, Frank counted to three, and did the most fearful thing his mind could endure. He released his death grip and twisted around and grabbed the rope while falling towards the rushing water. He held on tight while trying to put his feet back on the lower ledge. To his horror he heard the limb snap and the rope suddenly went limp. Down he went into the hellish current. His mind told him that this might be the end as he splashed into the frothing river and went underwater.

Nicole yelled and grabbed the broken tree limb as it slithered past her toward the ledge. Gripping it tightly, she dug her heels into the soft mud and held on.

Frank, being swept downstream, was about to abandon the rope when he felt it stiffen. As the current held him under, he wrapped the rope around his waist and felt his body being lifted back to the surface.

Up on top, Nicole quickly wrapped her end of the rope around the tree trunk. By using the trunk as a fulcrum, she struggled as she pulled the rope, hand over hand. Soon, excess rope began to gather on the ground around her feet. She kept pulling, hoping it wasn't too late. Her efforts paid off when she saw an exhausted Frank, coughing up water, put his hands up over the ledge. She ran over and helped boost him onto solid ground.

Lying on the upper ledge again, Frank breathed heavily, "I promise, I'll never say women are the weaker sex again."

"I'll remind you if you do," Nicole said, smiling for the first time tonight. "My arms felt as if they were being pulled out of their sockets. But what a fish I caught."

After they had rested, Frank and Nicole backtracked to the grotto to check the conditions of the agent and Wilson. Surprisingly, they found the FBI agent sitting in the rain in an upright position.

As Helen listened to their story about Fenton, she griped about the bulletproof vests stopping bullets but not cracked ribs. "I think the impact from the last shot he fired into me did the number on the ribs," she said. "Of course, I should be happy he didn't give me a head shot liked that poor fellow over there," pointing to Wilson's body.

Frank and Nicole helped the agent to her feet and assisted her in her slow painful walk up the hill to the parking area.

Along the way, Nicole promised Frank that she would never doubt him again. Except, of course, whenever he selects escape routes.

"Hey, I was right, the highway was in that direction. Was it my fault the river got in the way?"

49

The next morning at ten Nicole heard the doorbell ring. She leaned over and shook a sleeping Frank. "Someone's at the door. Your turn."

Frank slowly lifted himself up on his elbows. "Since when did we start taking turns?"

"Now," Nicole replied as she pulled the covers over her head. "My body is too bruised and sore to be a gracious hostess today. Be the good husband that I saved last night and see who's at the door."

"I guess you're going to hold that over me for the duration of our marriage."

"You betcha," Nicole mumbled.

Frank slipped on a robe and slippers and ambled down the stairs and opened the front door.

A man behind a bunch of flowers peered out at Frank. "This is my way to apologize to you and your wife," Coffey said.

"Thanks, but couldn't you have come a little later?" Frank asked. "We're still recovering from last night."

"Sorry, I have a flight back to Washington at noon and I wanted to give you the news about your buddy Fenton."

Frank instantly became alert. "Don't tell me you can't find his body? That maybe he's alive?"

"No. It's good news." Coffey said. "Sheriff's deputies found the body at daybreak five miles downstream."

Nicole came down the stairs in her robe. "I heard that. You mean this time, it's really all over?"

"Yes ma'am," he said, handing the flowers to Nicole. "He won't be bothering you or anyone anymore."

"For all his efforts, he only ended up with a swim in the Pedernales River," Frank said sarcastically.

"How is Helen?" Nicole inquired. "If it hadn't been for her, Frank and I would have been killed."

Coffey nodded. "Two of her ribs are cracked but outside of that, she's okay." He paused. "You know, before last night, she had been the butt of some our macho male agents jokes, but now she has gained their respect. She's a brave lady. And I might add, an awards ceremony is being planned for her as I speak."

"We would like to attend," Nicole said.

"I'll see that the department is informed of that," Coffey said approvingly. "Time to leave." He stopped and looked around, "You know, I really couldn't figure out why you would want to leave all of this."

Frank looked puzzled by Coffey's remark.

"Remember? I accused you of wanting to commit suicide for the insurance money."

"I can't blame you. Fenton really had me set up."

"Everybody should be so lucky to have a wife like yours."

"I couldn't agree more." Frank said as he put his arm around Nicole's shoulder and gave her a tight squeeze.